**The Earl's eyes,
usually so cold with contempt,
were alight with a strange fire.**

Suddenly she was in his arms, his hungry lips seeking hers in a ruthless, bruising kiss. . . .

Aurora was frozen in horror and shock. Despite herself, she felt her body respond to the consuming force of his desire. For one split second time stood still as her heart answered his unspoken call. . . .

Pride and memory returned. "How dare you, my lord!" she gasped. And the Earl, as if recollecting himself, flung her away with a cruel gesture of disdain.

Dear Reader:

After more than one year of publication, SECOND CHANCE AT LOVE has a lot to celebrate. Not only has it become firmly established as a major line of paperback romances, but response from our readers also continues to be warm and enthusiastic. Your letters keep pouring in—and we love receiving them. We're getting to know you—your likes and dislikes—and want to assure you that your contribution does make a difference.

As we work hard to offer you better and better SECOND CHANCE AT LOVE romances, we're especially gratified to hear that you, the reader, are rating us higher and higher. After all, our success depends on *you*. We're pleased that you enjoy our books and that you appreciate the extra effort our writers and staff put into them. Thanks for spreading the good word about SECOND CHANCE AT LOVE and for giving us your loyal support. Please keep your suggestions and comments coming!

With warm wishes,

Ellen Edwards

Ellen Edwards
SECOND CHANCE AT LOVE
The Berkley/Jove Publishing Group
200 Madison Avenue
New York, NY 10016

Second Chance at Love
REGENCY

DOUBLE DECEPTION
AMANDA TROY

**SECOND CHANCE AT LOVE
BOOK**

- 1 -

"I CANNOT LEAD the life of a sedate dowager," moaned Lady Lanville. "I am only eight and twenty. I must have some diversion. But what can I do—in my straitened circumstances?"

Aurora Marshingham smiled to herself at her cousin's exaggerated complaints. A tall, statuesque young woman, she was sitting in an armchair opposite her hostess. Lady Lanville was reclining that spring morning on a satin sofa in the yellow salon of her mansion in Berkeley Square.

In contrast to Lavinia Lanville's elegant blue robe, Aurora's gown was of a well-worn, serviceable green crepe; and if her bright auburn hair was fashionably dressed—piled on top of her head and allowed to fall in thick curls on either side of her face—it was not due to a maid's skillful hands but her own. At twenty-three, she was already responsible for the future of her two younger sisters—with little hope of providing properly for them.

"Attending the masquerade would be diverting," continued Lavinia. "I don't recollect when I last attended one." She gave a pathetic little sigh. "Ah, you don't know what it is to be without funds of one's own, to be obliged to give an account of every trifling expenditure."

1

Aurora's good humor kept her from protesting as her deep blue eyes traveled about the expensively furnished room. She noted the gold brocade draperies, the yellow-and-gold satin sofas and upholstered chairs, the white marble mantel, and the lustrous chandelier suspended from the ornamented ceiling. Penury indeed! Her generous mouth twisted into a smile. "Indeed, ma'am?" she said dryly. "I have been without funds these many years."

"Oh, in Yorkshire. *That* doesn't signify. Country living is so much simpler." Lady Lanville plied her fan. "While you were staying in Treeton Hall, you were your own mistress, running the household for your poor late papa; and though I'm sure you were obliged to penny-pinch, you could get by well enough. And while your stay with Aunt Martha must have been irksome to someone like yourself, you still were not obliged to spend large sums on hats and dresses and such. London *modistes* are exceedingly expensive, and here one must dress in the latest fashion if one doesn't wish to appear a dowd."

Aurora gave an inward sigh. "I am persuaded Lord Roxton gives you a handsome allowance, and he provides well for the children too," she commented.

"Oh, the children. To be sure. After all, *their* papa was his beloved brother. *Me* he never liked above half. He only tolerates me."

"I cannot allow it to be true. Surely you must be mistaken," Aurora said.

"But you don't know Roxton. You, with your generosity and kind heart—not that that was not the height of folly to persuade me to take on that wrenched girl as a kitchen maid. I can't afford to hire more servants."

"But she was starving," Aurora replied quietly.

"To be sure. But if you were to foist every starving waif on my household, I would soon be reduced to like poverty myself. But that's neither here nor there. Oh, Roxton is a hard man, with no sensibility, no consideration for someone with a delicate state of nerves and a constitution less robust than his own. How lucky you are to enjoy such excellent health yourself."

Aurora inclined her head in agreement. "Indeed, I am.

For who would want to hire someone prone to palpitations and vapors."

The widow made an impatient clicking sound with her tongue. "Pray don't tell me you still hold on to that nonsensical notion of seeking a post. Lord Treeton's daughter, a governess or a schoolmistress, looking after some spoiled brats." She shuddered dramatically.

"There is nothing wrong with honest labor," said Aurora, her head high. "Nothing to be ashamed of."

"But don't you wish to be wed, Aurora?" Lady Lanville asked.

Aurora grew pensive for a moment. Wish to be wed? Oh, yes, she had wished to be wed—once. Very much so. To a handsome dashing officer who had been visiting his uncle in Yorkshire. . . . She had always said she would marry only for love. So had Waldo—until he had discovered that Aurora's papa had died almost penniless. Aurora had discovered the bitter truth that the love she held for Waldo was not enough to keep him. She had believed she would never get over the disillusionment and the pain of Waldo's perfidy. Now she had a certain mistrust of all men's motives and doubted if love, real love, would come her way again. Strange that the memory of Waldo, once so painful, now evoked in her only a faint feeling of regret . . .

She was startled by Lavinia's voice repeating the question. Aurora answered slowly. "Yes, I would like to be wed—if I were to fall in love with a man and he with me. And only then. But one must be realistic. There is precious little chance of that happening to me."

"You never know when you might meet with an eligible bachelor who would take a fancy to you. You have a great deal of countenance. And that brings me back to the masquerade. Don't you agree it is a perfectly splendid notion?"

"But I don't have a costume," Aurora objected.

"We shall wear dominoes. I have already procured a blue one for you. Oh, and you can wear my blue dress, the one that I don't think becomes me after all. At least if you wear it, it won't go to waste."

Aurora eyed her cousin dubiously. "If I contrive to fit

into it, I shall be much obliged to you."

"Oh, I am persuaded you will. Besides, it's of no consequence if it isn't an exact fit. The domino will cover most of your gown. I shall wear my cherry-red gown, the one with the silver fringe, with a red domino." Lavinia chattered happily. "Roxton says it isn't fitting for me to wear the dress now, but I'm too young to play a widow on the shelf. But of course *he* has no sensibility at all. Odious, overbearing man."

During her short stay in Berkeley Square, Aurora had heard a great deal of criticism placed on the head of my Lord Roxton—a man so autocratic he would not allow Lavinia, the children's own mother, to arrange for the schooling of his niece and nephew; Lord Roxton held the purse strings and Lord Roxton was very tightfisted—even if it wasn't his own money he was doling out to her but his late brother's. As the head of the family, Lord Roxton was horribly rich, yet he begrudged a poor lonely widow a few groats for some fripperies to cheer up her days. Aurora heard so much that she became quite curious to see the ogre for herself.

"And you can wear the pearls with it too, for I shall be wearing my rubies." Lavinia's high-pitched voice cut in on Aurora's musings.

"What? Oh, no—not the Roxton pearls. I couldn't. Lord Roxton might object," Aurora persisted.

"He won't know anything about it. He's not expected back in town for a sennight. Besides, he can't object to my wearing them, and you are my friend and my cousin."

Your poor relation, thought Aurora with slight bitterness, upon whom you choose to bestow your largesse. Yet Lavinia wasn't a bad woman—if one disregarded her frequent spasms and vapors, which always seemed to come on when she was faced with something unpleasant.

"Then that is all settled. Oh, we shall have a famous time of it, I'm sure," exclaimed Lady Lanville, well satisfied with her plan.

"But we cannot go there without an escort," said Aurora.

Lady Lanville's face suddenly acquired a sly look. "As a matter of fact, a gentleman friend of mine has kindly offered to accompany me to the masquerade. But it will not do for you to be without a partner, so we shall ask Albert. I have sent round to Brook Street, and he should be here presently."

As if to confirm her words, the butler entered to announce the arrival of Lord Deberough, the Earl of Roxton's younger brother and heir.

"Desire his lordship to come up immediately, Stobbins," Lavinia said, becoming even more animated.

The butler bowed and withdrew, and a moment later a slim youth with fair locks and blue eyes, dressed in an elegant coat of blue superfine, entered the room.

The Viscount Deberough, who was twenty-two years of age though he looked much younger, sketched a deep bow to both ladies. His eyes showed frank admiration as he lingered a trifle longer than necessary over Aurora's hand. Aurora experienced an uncomfortable feeling of displeasure. It was not in her design to have the viscount fall in love with her. He seemed to her a boy. If anything, she would have wished that such a fate had befallen her younger sister Priscilla.

But nothing could have induced Priscilla to pay a visit to Lady Lanville. Some foolish notion she had taken into her head, fancying herself in love with a soldier—a penniless squire's second son. To be sure, Bertram was a fine, upstanding young man and—unlike Waldo—sincere in his feelings toward Priscilla. But at nineteen he was much too young to set up his own household.

While as a rule Aurora objected to a loveless marriage, she recognized that practical matters had to be taken into consideration. So when Lady Lanville, a distant cousin whom Aurora did not know at all, had invited one of the Marshingham girls to stay with her at her fashionable town house in Berkeley Square, Aurora had not hesitated long. Priscilla wouldn't go, and Adelina was still in the schoolroom. This, thought Aurora, would be her opportunity to try to establish herself as a schoolmistress or a governess. Lady Lanville enjoyed a wide circle of friends and might be able to help her find a suitable position. But Lady Lanville had proven not at all desirous of bringing this about.

"And how can I be of service to you both?" asked the obliging viscount, seating himself upon the sofa and crossing his legs, which were elegantly clad in fawn-colored pantaloons.

"Aurora and I have decided to attend the masquerade at the opera house," Lavinia explained. "Aurora has never been to one, you see, and it would be a great treat for her. She needs an escort, and I'm sure you would not mind performing this service."

The viscount inclined his head. "I would be most happy to, but . . . Lavinia, it is not quite the thing to go to one of these affairs. I am persuaded Roxton would not like it above half."

"Roxton, Roxton, Roxton!" the widow shrieked, clapping her hands to her ears. "I declare, if I hear his odious name once more I shall have one of my worst spasms!"

The viscount glanced at Aurora. "Do you also wish it, ma'am?"

Aurora shrugged. "I do not think we can come to any trouble if we keep our masks on."

She could have laughed at the youth's expression, so clearly were his thoughts mirrored there. The more he thought of the idea, the better he liked it. To dance with Aurora in the intimate and slightly clandestine atmosphere of a masked ball . . .

"You will escort us, won't you?" Lavinia asked eagerly.

"With the greatest pleasure on earth—as long as neither of you will let Roxton hear of it, or I shall receive a rare trimming from him for abetting you in such impropriety."

Lavinia's pale-green eyes sparkled. "Oh, thank you, Albert. I am much obliged to you. I knew you would not fail us."

The viscount frowned. "The only thing is, I can only dance with one of you at a time, while the other would be obliged to sit unattended in the box. Not at all the thing. And I don't like to—"

"Oh, don't worry about *me*," interrupted Lavinia. "I shall have Alphonsus to keep me company."

"What!" The viscount seemed suddenly stricken with dismay. "No. No, really, Lavinia. You can't. Not when Roxton particularly desired you not to have anything to do with that scoundrel."

"He is no such thing. A flirt merely."

"Besides being over forty years of age."

"What's that got to do with it?" Lavinia retorted.

"And inclined to stoutness," the viscount added.

"He is not."

Aurora listened to this interchange in lively astonishment. Apparently this Alphonsus, whoever he was, stood high in Lady Lanville's favor. "Who is Alphonsus?" she managed to interject. "Your particular friend?"

Lavinia blushed but said airily, "Oh, he is Alphonsus Fant, Baron Style. Perfectly respectable, of good breeding—he is everywhere received—and a onetime friend of the family."

"No, no, *not* of the family, Lavinia," the viscount disagreed. "Not now, anyway. That is coming it much too strong."

"Well, a friend of my late husband's and *my* friend," Lavinia corrected.

The viscount's face became stern and mulish. "I cannot agree to your going out with him," he said with unwonted resolution. "I am responsible for you while James is not here."

"Oh, fiddle! He knows you can't control me and won't hold it against you—*if* he ever finds out about it, which he won't."

She turned to Aurora. "Alphonsus is a pet even though he is getting on in years. But he and Roxton are at odds and Roxton positively forbids me to keep company with him. Which is perfectly ridiculous since I am not a green miss. I'll be dashed if I will obey him when he's not even in town. And I'll seize any opportunity of cutting a caper."

"But, Lavinia—you are a widow with two children," Lord Deberough exclaimed.

Lady Lanville flushed a dull red. "You think I'm not behaving as I ought, do you? Don't *you* speak to me of propriety, Albert. You, who but a short while ago, was squiring Lady Clara all over town in the teeth of Roxton's opposition? He dislikes her as much as he does Alphonsus. And she is at least eight years older than you."

Now it was the young viscount's turn to redden. "That's neither here nor there. We were talking of the impropriety of your going to the masquerade with Alphonsus. And you don't know everything there is to know about Alphonsus," the viscount suggested darkly.

"Oh, yes, I do. Just because he is a gamester, you all think he induced Will to become a gamester too. But it was no such thing. Will frequented the gaming hells before he started going with Alphonsus. But I won't stand here and be lectured by you!" she concluded, stamping her foot. "If you don't go with us, we shall both go with Alphonsus."

"But I can't permit—"

Lady Lanville fell back on the sofa and began to fan herself. "If you keep on in this fashion, you shall bring on one of my worst spasms...."

"But—"

"Oh, Aurora, dear," the widow moaned in a moribund voice, "pray, fetch me my vinaigrette. Ring the bell and desire Bellman to bring me some hartshorn and water. Oh, I fear I am getting my palpitations.... Oh, Albert, you obstinate, odious man, you are making me ill, quite ill."

The young viscount seemed irresolute and unhappy.

Aurora gave him an encouraging smile. "You might as well give in, my lord, for you know you shan't withstand her for long. And we shall have her drumming her feet pretty soon, if you don't."

"Aurora!" shrieked Lady Lanville, sitting up with a jerk and casting a reproachful look on her cousin. Then she immediately fell back on the cushions and closed her eyes. "My vinaigrette, pray, Aurora...."

Aurora took the bottle from a side table and handed it to her. Lady Lanville uncorked it and began to sniff at it delicately.

"Oh, very well," the viscount capitulated. "Have your own way."

The vinaigrette slowly lowered. "You will go with us? I knew you wouldn't be so disobliging as to refuse."

"Yes, well. But mind we leave before the unmasking. Is Alphonsus taking you up in his carriage?"

"Yes. He is to call for me here."

"Roxton will be furious when he discovers he has set foot in this house."

"It is not Roxton's house, thank God."

"Yes, but—oh, very well. I just hope Alphonsus takes

good care of you. Those affairs are not at all the thing."

"Don't worry. You just take care of Aurora, for I shall be too busy to bother about her," Lavinia pronounced.

"I shall be very happy to do so." The viscount's eyes sparkled as he raised them to Aurora's face. Aurora gave another inward sigh. She ought not to go with him, for that would encourage him in his infatuation. But the temptation to attend a masquerade was too strong to resist.

- 2 -

THE EVENING OF the masquerade began auspiciously enough.
The color and the glitter of the opera house, the merriment
within its splendid walls, appealed to Aurora. The crimson
draperies, the brilliant chandeliers, and the large stage, now
turned into a dance floor full of twirling ladies and gentlemen
in costumes and dominoes, presented a vibrant, festive spectacle that was reflected in her own mood. And as it had
been some time since she had attended her last country ball,
she delighted in dancing with Lord Albert, the Viscount
Deberough—an excellent dancer.

Even the viscount's ardor and the increasingly improper
behavior of the crowd failed to dampen her enjoyment. From
the safety of her box and in the company of Lord Albert,
she could take pleasure in the colorful spectacle without any
qualms.

Then events took a turn for the worse. Aurora had become quite hot and thirsty and begged Lord Albert to fetch
her some lemonade. He went to procure it—and did not
return. And since the Baron of Style and Lady Lanville had
disappeared shortly after the four of them had entered the
opera house, Aurora was left alone in the box, unprotected.
After waiting awhile, she went in search of Lord Albert; but

she was repeatedly accosted by strolling gentlemen, who must have imbibed something stronger than lemonade. To escape from them, the young lady was obliged to return to her box.

Still, although the box was on the second tier, she was constantly embarrassed by inquisitive bucks who mistook her box for theirs and were reluctant to leave it, forcing her to fight off their advances. This was not her notion of a rare treat, and her dissatisfaction and indignation mounted.

At last, after what seemed to Aurora an interminable time, Lady Lanville and the baron returned. Lavinia appeared to be suffering from an agitation of the nerves, for she was trembling violently and kept pressing her hands to her bosom. After collapsing on a seat, and before Aurora had a chance to protest the shabby treatment her companions had accorded her, she grasped Aurora by the hand and whispered in failing accents, "You must help me, Aurora. You must, or I am undone. If Roxton finds me here, I have sunk myself below reproach in his eyes. He will pack me off to Roxton Hall, and I simply cannot—cannot—bear the country."

Aurora felt the wind taken out of the sails of her indignation. "But why should he find out?" she asked, bewildered. "He is away from town."

"No, he isn't. He came back home to Mount Street unexpectedly. And—and—Oh, I feel my spasms coming on." Falling back against the cushion, she began to fan herself, bereft of speech.

"The thing is, Miss Marshingham," said the baron, "he has somehow discovered that Lady Lanville has come to the masquerade in my company. And you must have heard in what aversion he holds me. Please do help us."

Aurora could not fathom why the earl should dislike the baron so excessively, although she herself did not care much for this stocky, florid-faced dandy. How could Lavinia ever have become enamoured of this scented, middle-aged exquisite with his ornate quizzing glass, his many seals, fobs, and jeweled rings? His countenance held in it nothing remarkable either; but apparently his indifferent hazel eyes and his wide mouth were to Lavinia's liking.

To be sure, his brown locks were brushed into the fashionable Brutus style, his shirt collars were monstrously high and stiffly starched, and his cravat was expertly tied—all signs denoting a Tulip, the veriest Pink of the Pinks, so she had been told. But she was not partial to gaudy raiment in a man.

Lavinia now regained her voice. "You *must* help us, Aurora," she begged urgently. "Take my domino and go onto the dance floor with Alphonsus. Roxton will think it is I, but as soon as he asks you to unmask, he'll discover his mistake. By that time I shall be well on the way to Berkeley Square. I've charged Albert to see about the carriage. He'll bring me home."

Aurora stared at her with lively astonishment. "Surely Lord Roxton will not come rushing after you here," she managed to say at last.

"Oh, yes, he will. It would be just like him to come rushing to this 'den of iniquity' to rescue me from the clutches of a villain. Oh, I am getting one of my spasms—"

"Not until we have the matter settled," snapped the baron, in a very unloverlike manner. "Now, Lavinia, compose yourself."

Aurora's indignation at last found expression. "I beg your pardon, Lavinia—Lady Lanville—but why should I put myself in a scrape by getting you out of it? You had promised me an evening of rare entertainment, instead of which I found myself sitting alone in the box, fending off inquisitive bucks. And where—where the devil has Lord Albert gone to? I desired him to fetch me some lemonade and he disappeared."

"I—I am afraid it is my fault," Lavinia said in a small voice. "I met him in the saloon and I, that is, we, promised to bring you the lemonade, while he had a short conversation with Lady Clara."

"Which turned into quite a long conversation," said Aurora crossly. "How could Lord Albert behave with such lack of—" Abruptly she remembered Lavinia telling her that Lady Clara was the female whom Lord Albert had been enamoured of before he had met herself. But that still was not an excuse for his deserting her in such a fashion.

"Oh, Aurora, this is all to no purpose now," fretted

Lavinia. "You must help me out of this fix. It doesn't matter if Roxton sees *you* with Alphonsus. You are not his favorite brother's wife. Why should he care a button what company you keep? And it would save me from a horrid fate."

Which sounded perfectly true. Only . . . Aurora did not particularly like Lord Style. As she stood there, indecision and vexation mirrored on her lovely face, Lavinia moaned.

"Albert can come for you later, or Alphonsus can bring you home. It doesn't signify. But I must escape before I'm discovered. Oh, I feel *ill*. If only I had my smelling salts with me. Aurora, say you will help me."

Abruptly Lavinia jumped to her feet and with feverish haste began to divest herself of her domino.

Aurora heaved an impatient sigh. "Oh, very well, I'll go along with this charade." She slipped off her own domino and threw it on a chair. "But I must say that I am very much put out by the whole thing."

"You are put out!" cried Lady Lanville, much affronted, while she slipped on Aurora's domino.

"Why can't Lord Style take you home?" Aurora asked.

"What! And have Roxton find us together? If he chances to see me and Albert driving up, we can always say we have been to some party. But if he should spot me with Alphonsus . . ." She shuddered dramatically.

At that moment a red-faced and embarrassed Lord Albert returned, stammering abject apologies to Aurora. But Lavinia did not allow him to express his profound regret at having cavalierly deserted the lady in his charge. After extracting from Aurora a promise never to divulge the truth about this affair to Lord Roxton, she whisked him out of the box.

Aurora did not like this turn of events, but deciding to make the best of it, she allowed the baron to lead her onto the dance floor. The masquerade had turned into a boisterous romp. More and more flashy bucks, now quite the worse for wear, were ogling and accosting the ladies unashamedly; the dancing couples on the stage were behaving with a complete lack of decorum.

"Lord Style, pray, take me home," Aurora said. "Remaining any longer would serve no purpose. I am persuaded

Lord Roxton is not likely to come dashing here after Lady Lanville."

In response, the Baron of Style's grip tightened about her waist. "But we cannot be quite sure of that, my dear Miss Marshingham. Come, do not look so displeased. You dance divinely." His hazel eyes twinkled roguishly.

Aurora fought off the temptation to tread on his toes. "I dislike being jostled about. Pray have the goodness to convey me back to Berkeley Square."

"Ah, no, no. Surely you cannot be so cruel as to think me an indifferent partner. I consider dancing one of my few accomplishments."

Aurora sighed. She had to agree with him; he was an even better dancer than Lord Albert. But that was the only thing about him she approved of.

"I have no fault to find with your dancing, Lord Style," she said, trying to be civil, "but no matter how well one may dance, it is impossible to enjoy oneself in this crowd. And I am persuaded most of these people are three parts bosky."

The baron was about to utter something when, abruptly, they were startled by a harsh voice heard above the noise of the crowd and music. "Ah, there you are. I could scarcely believe it was true!" Pushing his way toward them was a tall, powerful man with short dark hair and an arrogant jaw.

The next moment a hand was clamped roughly on Aurora's shoulder. That same cold voice exclaimed, "This time you have gone too far, Lavinia. Style, unhand the lady to my care at once!"

- 3 -

THE BARON'S ARM tightened around Aurora's waist. "I'm afraid you are making a big mistake, old fellow, for which I shall receive your apology."

The man gave an unpleasant bark of laughter. "I? Apologize to you? You must have taken leave of your senses. Unhand her this instant!"

"I am afraid, I am very much afraid you are laboring under a misapprehension, my lord," Baron Style said urbanely. "This is not Lady Lanville but a particular friend of mine. And you are causing her a great deal of embarrassment with your uncouth behavior. I must request you to leave us immediately and stop annoying the lady. You may take my word for it. She is not Lady Lanville."

"Not Lavinia?" cried Lord Roxton. "Of course it is Lavinia. This is her domino, isn't it?" There was contempt and incredulity and yet a trace of uneasiness in the scornful voice. "However, we shall put it to the test. Madam, pray be so kind as to remove your mask."

"I will not," Aurora said in muffled accents. She was beginning to enjoy herself. What a setdown it would be for this imperious man when he discovered his mistake. At the

17

same time she could now better understand and indeed even sympathize with Lavinia. The earl seemed not to have the slightest regard for his sister-in-law's feelings, to scold her thus in public. She scanned his tall figure with great interest.

James Oliver Lanville, the sixth Earl of Roxton, was a handsome man, but of a stern countenance with his lips set in an uncompromising line and the hardest gray eyes she had ever encountered. Lavinia had told her he was thirty-five years of age, but he looked older. Apparently he had not deemed it necessary to wear evening clothes to such a "vulgar" affair as this, or perhaps he'd no time to change into something more appropriate, for his only token of the occasion was a black domino carried over his arm.

Nevertheless, his elegant blue, long-tailed coat molded to his broad powerful shoulders, his close-fitting fawn pantaloons which set off his shapely legs to advantage, and his gleaming Hessian boots with the swinging gold tassels far outshone the gaudy appearance of Lord Style and that of the other costumed gentlemen. His white muslin neck-cloth, though exquisitely tied in intricate folds, was not as stiffly starched as that of the baron, nor were his shirt-collar points as high as those of Lord Style or even Lord Albert, testifying to the fact that he disliked foppishness. His only adornments were a quizzing glass, hung on a black ribbon round his neck, and a ruby signet ring on his finger. He was an impressive man in the first stare of elegance and fashion, and he had an air of self-consequence that showed he was used to having his way.

"Madam, I am not trifling. I am in earnest. Remove your mask this instant," repeated the earl.

Aurora shook her head, barely suppressing a giggle. The man was begging for a setdown.

The next moment she gave a light cry as the mask was ruthlessly torn from her face. But the consternation in the eyes of the earl more than compensated her for his rudeness. Blank astonishment spread over his face, to be followed by a rigid look. He gave her a small bow. "It seems I must beg your pardon, madam," he said stiffly. "Apparently I was working under a misapprehension. Pray accept my apologies."

Aurora inclined her head an eighth of an inch.

The earl turned to Lord Style. "I must felicitate you on your choice of a new companion. She is quite a notch above Clara. Much more comely."

Aurora, unaccountably pleased that he found her attractive, felt her pulse quicken at his words. In spite of his forbidding and rude manner, she saw this handsome gentleman as the very embodiment of masculine strength and found herself pleasurably stirred by the encounter.

But she was mystified by his remark. Who was Clara? Did he perchance mean Lady Clara? Lady Clara? But she was, or had been, the viscount's inamorata!

"Though I hardly can commend *your* taste, ma'am," the earl was saying with another, ironic bow in her direction.

Abruptly his eyes narrowed with suspicion and anger. The taut line above his mouth hardened, and his countenance assumed a grim expression. His hand shot out and lifted the pearl necklace hanging around her neck, causing Aurora to almost lose her balance. Only his hold on her shoulder steadied her.

He studied the necklace's distinctive diamond clasp. "How is it that you are wearing the Roxton pearls, madam?" he asked in an ominous tone. "Answer me that, madam. Answer me!" As Aurora's face registered dismay, he turned to the baron. "Can you explain this to me, pray?"

The baron only shrugged. "Don't ask me to account for a lady's toilette. That is beyond me. I certainly had nothing to do with it."

"How came you by *my* pearls? Answer me, girl!" seethed the earl.

Aurora recovered quickly from her discomposure. "Unhand me, my lord. You are forgetting yourself. We have not even been introduced. If you cannot behave yourself with a semblance of decorum—"

"Hell and the devil!" thundered the earl. "Are you going to preach to *me—you*—when you stole the Roxton pearls? And that dress. That is Lavinia's. Did you come by it the same way?"

Aurora stiffened in his iron grip, then drew herself up. Her cheeks reddened; her lively blue eyes flashed with indignation. "It was no such thing. Lady Lanville was kind enough to lend me the dress and the pearls."

"What?" the earl stared at her incredulously, but he relinquished his hold on her. "How came you to be so well acquainted with Lady Lanville?"

"I am Aurora Marshingham, my lord. And I am at present staying with her ladyship. As for the necklace—I am sorry you are displeased. I surmised you would be and indeed ventured to say as much to Lady Lanville, but she assured me she had leave to wear it—"

"She—yes; but to bestow—Did you say *staying* with her? Marshingham . . ." He looked thunderstruck for a moment. The grim expression about his mouth and in his eyes deepened. Then he let out a long breath. "So, you are the jade who has set her cap at Albert. Fancying to be the future Countess of Roxton, what? And I gave you credit for being merely an impoverished female desiring to better her position in life. Instead you are this scoundrel Style's new accomplice. Clara's lures did not prove strong enough to overcome my opposition, so he sent out somebody young and fresh to snare the boy. It is a pity that such a lovely face should belong to a jezebel, in league with a damned blackguard. I see I was right in posting to town the moment I was informed of the state of affairs in Berkeley Square."

Aurora stared at him aghast, bewildered, and outraged. That *he*, that *anyone*, should dare speak thus to her! Her eyes blazing with wrath, she spat at him, "How dare you insult me so, calling me such names! You shall rue those words, my lord, bitterly. But don't expect me to pardon you. Ever. No matter how you beg me to."

"*I* beg your pardon? Beg pardon of a Cyprian and a jade? By God, you do give yourself airs, girl. And by God, you are magnificent in your scorn. I can see why Albert lost his heart—"

"I don't thank you for the compliment, my lord."

"I didn't intend it as such."

"Oh, you are insufferable!" With a violent jerk of her hand, Aurora undid the clasp and thrust the necklace at Lord Roxton. "Here, take your odious pearls, and—and go to the devil with them!" she exploded. She turned and began to push her way through a curious and appreciative crowd.

"A termagant, eh?" she heard the earl say. Then his hand clamped forcibly on her arm.

She tried to wrench free. "Let go, my lord. I desire to return home."

"And so you shall. In my curricle."

"No."

The baron, finding his voice at last, sprang to her defense. "The lady came with me and I shall drive her home."

"Oh, no, you won't. And if you don't want me to plant you a facer, you had better remove yourself at once."

The baron stood his ground. "My lord, you shall answer me for this insult," he said with ponderous dignity.

"You mean you will call me out? Don't be ridiculous. You are a very bad shot, and I never miss my mark. Come, wench."

"Lord Style!" Aurora cried in despair.

The baron shrugged. "Alas, you had better go with him, or we shall have a very disgusting, vulgar brawl on our hands. I do regret the incident enormously and humbly beg your pardon."

"Oh, *pshaw,*" Aurora exclaimed thoroughly irritated. "Why don't you knock him down?" But as soon as she had said the words, she realized how ridiculous the suggestion was. She shook her head. "No, it won't answer."

"Just so," the earl said dryly. "Will you come with me willingly, or shall I drag you from here by force?"

"I will go," Aurora said through clenched teeth. "If you insist on something so improper. But I don't see why Lord Style cannot accompany me home."

"I will not have that scoundrel on my doorstep."

"But Berkeley Square is not *your* doorstep."

He seemed to be taken aback. Then his expression turned still more forbidding. "It is my late brother's house, and I shall protect his honor to the best of my ability."

"You—*you* talking of honor!" stormed Aurora as he was guiding her toward the exit. "You don't know the meaning of the word. No man of honor would inflict such pain and embarrassment on a lady in a public place."

He gave a contemptuous laugh. "What? Those drunk cits and their fancies? Surely you're not paying any heed to them. And no Lady of Quality would show her face here. Members of the *ton* don't attend opera masquerades, my wench."

"Don't call me 'my wench,'" snapped Aurora, drawing herself up. "I am Miss Marshingham to you."

He inclined his head an inch in an ironic bow. "Very prettily done, that outraged expression. You ought to be on the stage, Miss Marshingham. But you are wasting your talents on this crowd. They would not appreciate you even if they were sober."

Aurora was speechless. It seemed nothing she said could convince him that she was not a woman of easy virtue—merely because he mistook her for Lord Style's particular lady friend, which false notion she had foolishly agreed to foster in him. It was to be expected that he would not look upon her with favor, believing her to be a friend of the man whom he detested.

But she certainly did not expect such a violent reaction on his part. The only way she could correct his misapprehension would be to tell him the truth. And that she could not do, for she had promised Lavinia she would not. Besides, it was unforgivable of him to jump to such a conclusion when he knew absolutely nothing about her. That was being prejudicial in the worst way. Even if the Baron of Style were all that Lord Roxton accused him of being, it did not necessarily follow that a lady seen in his company was cut of the same cloth.

Furthermore, what was all this buisness of the Baron and Lady Clara's trying to entrap the viscount? She could understand a woman wanting to marry Lord Albert, but why would the baron abet such a scheme? What did Lord Roxton mean when he intimated that Lady Clara was Alphonsus's accomplice? All these questions and the different emotions battling in her breast made Aurora's head whirl.

In high dudgeon, her lips clamped shut, she sat beside him in the curricle—thankful for the absence of his groom—while he expertly guided a pair of spirited grays toward Berkeley Square. In spite of her dislike of him, she could not help being strongly aware of his powerful body so close to her own. Nor could she help admitting to herself that he was an excellent whip, for though his mouth was rigid and the muscle of his cheek quivered from time to time, betraying his suppressed anger, his hands on the ribbons were steady and calm. He too maintained a stony silence, until they arrived in Berkeley Square, when he jumped down from his curricle, made as if to help her to alight, then changed his mind. "You can climb down without my assist," he said curtly.

Aurora, seething with indignation at this further proof of his lack of manners, prepared to alight by herself. Thankfully she was conversant with sporting vehicles and managed to get down without embarrassing herself. But apparently she was not quick enough for his lordship.

"Pray, ma'am, make haste. I must beg leave to have a word with you at once. And with Lady Lanville."

Aurora's brows went up at this sudden show of civility; then seeing the open front door and Lavinia's butler standing on the threshold, she perceived that his sudden politeness was for the benefit of the servants. And his promise of a word with her and Lavinia boded no good.

"I have nothing to say to you, my lord," she declared, sweeping ahead of him into the house. "I am tired and I desire to retire to my chamber."

"Nevertheless, you will oblige me with a few minutes of your time," he said between his teeth. "I shall give you half an hour to compose yourself and to change, after which you shall join me and Lavinia in the yellow salon."

Aurora did not deign to answer him—but didn't dare refuse him either. She fairly flew up the wide staircase, fearing that her strong feelings would betray her in an unseemly display of temper in front of the servants. As she pushed open the door to her room, she observed the door to Lavinia's chamber closing softly. That scatterbrained, flighty widow! thought Aurora. She had certainly put them both in a fine fix. How would she be able to continue under her roof now? Still, Lord Roxton did not reside in Berkeley Square, and surely he could not forbid Lady Lanville to entertain a relative in her home. Oh, it was all such a dreadful muddle.

- 4 -

By the time Aurora had changed her borrowed ballgown for her own gown of mulled muslin and brushed her disheveled curls, she was composed enough to enter the yellow salon with a semblance of calm.

The earl was striding up and down the room, striking the palm of his hand with his gloves and generally presenting an impatient and exasperated state of mind. He whirled on Aurora as she entered. "Oh, there you are, madam. You took your time coming down." He glanced impatiently at his watch.

Aurora shrugged. "I am here now, am I not? But where is Lady Lanville?"

Lord Roxton uttered an exasperated oath. "In her chamber, prostrated with the vapors. The minute I taxed her with this matter, off she went into strong hysterics. And then swooned. The most tiresome female I have ever encountered. I hope, ma'am, you shall not enact me any similar Cheltenham tragedies."

Aurora made him a mocking curtsy. "Oh, pray, what would be the use of *that*, my lord? I have no audience, and you, I am persuaded, do not appreciate my talents."

The earl's eyes narrowed. "Impudent baggage." He inspected her briefly through his quizzing glass. "But you have spirit. Still, an adventuress must possess that quality to succeed—as you apparently have, with Albert."

"I collect it would be useless to protest that I never had nor have any designs on Lord Deberough," Aurora said coldly, "and that his attentions are as embarrassing to me as they are unwelcome."

"Quite useless. I saw the evidence to the contrary with my own eyes."

"What evidence?"

"Your friendship with Alphonsus," Roxton replied.

"My friendship with Baron Style has nothing to do with the viscount."

"Oh, hasn't it?" He gave her a penetrating glance. "Surely you're not thinking of catching Style for a husband. He hasn't a feather to fly with and you, from all accounts, are penniless too."

Aurora crossed to the yellow sofa and sank gracefully onto it. "It seems to me, my lord," she said with great deliberation, "that you are busying yourself overmuch with what is none of your affair. My relationship with Baron Style is not at all your concern." When he would have interrupted, she put up a hand. "Wait. Pray hear me out. As for her ladyship, you may censure her conduct as you wish, if she is a ninnyhammer as to let you do so. However, you have no right forbidding her to invite someone to stay with her, as I collect you mean to do. It suits my purpose to stay with Lady Lanville at present, and so I shall continue to reside here, your displeasure notwithstanding. If you do not like Lord Albert's seeing me, forbid him to call in Berkeley Square."

"You know damn well he wouldn't listen."

"But you hold his purse strings, at least until he is married."

"Yes. And I also hold Lavinia's purse strings. I can force her to throw you out of here," the earl said grimly.

"Oh, you would not punish her so severely. Why, she might be prostrated for a week. Besides, if you force me to leave town—for I can't afford to stay at a hotel or set up my own establishment—her ladyship will likely turn to the baron for consolation, and *that* would not suit you at all."

"No, by God, it wouldn't! But your entrapping Albert into marriage wouldn't suit me either!"

The earl took a turn about the room. "Do you ask me to believe that Style did not set you up as bait for Albert, that it was just a coincidence that you—Style's new mistress—"

"I beg your pardon," Aurora interrupted in an icy tone.

"His 'particular friend' then, if you prefer the term; it doesn't signify. Do you ask me to believe that you just happened to catch Albert's fancy? That it was just a coincidence that, when Style's previous lady love failed in her attempts at entrapping Albert into marriage against my wishes, you appeared on the scene? No, no, my girl, it won't wash. I won't swallow that."

Aurora stamped her foot. "I am not asking you to swallow anything. I am asking you to remove your obnoxious person from my sight. Since obviously you are incapable of intelligent conversation, there is nothing more to be said between us."

The cold gray eyes flashed with an ominous anger. "Oh, yes, there is, my girl," he said through his teeth. "Fine and mighty regal behavior for a Cyprian, ordering me—*me*—out of the room." He stepped up to the sofa, grasped Aurora by the shoulders, and gave her a good shake. The gesture, though provoking her wrath, made her again acutely conscious of his strength.

"I warn you, my wench," he continued, "keep your claws off Albert. And I might as well tell you now, I won't tolerate his marriage to you any more than I did countenance it to Clara."

Aurora's blue eyes blazed with fury. She jumped to her feet. "How dare you lay your hands on me, you uncouth boor, you overbearing, conceited, arrogant man. You think everyone will jump through your hoop. Well, you're very much mistaken. Lord Albert is of age, and he can do as he pleases. And it seems to me that it would be an excellent thing for him to marry me, for then he would be rid of you as his guardian or—or trustee, or whatever it is that gives

you control over his money. And don't think I couldn't
make him marry me—for I certainly could. And in the teeth
of your opposition too. I had no inclination to marry him—
for to me he's more of a puppy than a man—but by God,
sir, your insolent behavior makes me itch to do just that—
to spike your guns. And don't tell me I'm using cant phrases,
you shouldn't be surprised. After all, in your eyes I'm no
lady. Well, I may be no lady, but *you,* sir, are no gentleman!"

She had the satisfaction of seeing a dull flush spread over
his tanned cheeks, to be replaced immediately by a blaze
of anger. "Bravo, bravo! I repeat, madam, you should be
on the stage. You almost made me believe you were indeed
a Lady of Quality." He was glaring at her, and she glared
back at him, her bosom heaving, her blue eyes flashing with
the fire of outrage and injured dignity.

At that moment the Viscount Deberough burst into the
room. His boyish countenance was flushed and anxious.
"James, don't! I beg you!"

"What? What are you doing here, you whelp?" the earl
rounded on him.

"Bridget, the maid, came running to my lodgings with
the intelligence that you are about to murder Lavinia and
Aurora—Miss Marshingham. So I rushed here posthaste.
I shall tell you the whole truth. It can't be any worse
than—"

"Pray be silent, Lord Deberough," Aurora interrupted
quickly. "I beg you. There is nothing you can do that would
mend matters, and can you only make them worse. Lady
Lanville is already prostrated with hysterics, and I am not
in the least afraid of his lordship's temper tantrums."

"Temper tantrums? Temper tantrums!" The earl's hands
lifted, his fingers curled into claws as if to strangle her.

The viscount sprang forward, placing himself between
Aurora and the earl. "For God's sake, James!"

Aurora was slightly pale, but she stood her ground. "Do
not be alarmed, Lord Deberough. Lord Roxton shall not
harm me."

"No, he won't, for I shan't let him," said Lord Albert
fiercely.

"You shall not marry her, do you hear!" seethed the earl.

The viscount turned his mild blue eyes on his brother in surprise. "M-m-marry Aurora?" he gasped out.

The earl's eyes narrowed in a puzzled frown.

"You have been a trifle too precipitate, my lord," Aurora said with deep irony. "The Viscount Deberough, although enjoying my company, had thus far not declared his intentions. It is you yourself who is putting ideas into his head."

The earl seemed to be quite taken aback. "But . . . I was given the intelligence that—that you were quite smitten with this—this—"

Lord Albert drew himself up. "With Miss Marshingham, sir. And so I am. She is the dearest, the most beautiful creature I have ever seen. But I have known her only a short time and—and I do not even know if the lady reciprocates my feelings," he stammered, reddening. "I would deem it too soon to broach such a delicate subject to her."

"Oh, so you are playing hard to get, are you?" the earl accused Aurora.

"James, for heaven's sake," his brother interjected. "Miss Marshingham hasn't been staying in Berkeley Square more than a fortnight. We had hardly time to get well acquainted. And you are doing her grave injustice if you think she—she is out to entice me into marriage with her, for it is no such thing. She is a Lady of Quality, and I must ask you to beg her pardon for thinking otherwise. And how you came to reach such a conclusion has me in quite a puzzle."

The earl continued to regard his younger brother with a sour look. "A Lady of Quality would not make Alphonsus Fant her *particular friend*," he said dryly. But his wrath seemed to be burning itself out.

"Well, there you are wrong. Alphonsus is received in all the best houses, as you well know; besides, Aurora— Miss Marshingham—is n—"

"By your leave, Lord Deberough," Aurora interrupted in a decisive tone. "I can speak well for myself, and if I do not choose to do so, that is my own concern. Now do be good enough to leave us; for the greatest service you can do to me at present is not to try defending me."

"But—"

"Oh, have done, have done," the earl said abruptly in a weary voice. "It seems I have been misinformed into thinking the situation much more serious than it is. If you choose to engage in a flirtation with Miss Marshingham, that is no concern of mine; but were you to contemplate marriage with her, as you did with Lady Clara—"

"You cannot speak of Lady Clara and Miss Marshingham in the same breath," the viscount cried out with indignation. "Lady Clara is an excellent woman but—but—Miss Marshingham is of quite a different cut."

The earl regarded Aurora with a skeptical stare. "I wish I could believe you, but I very much fear it is no such thing. However, you have had my warning."

He approached the bell rope and tugged at it sharply.

"What are you going to do?" asked the viscount, rather alarmed.

"Do? I shall desire Stobbins to have my bedchamber made ready." He yawned. "I am fagged. And since I must have word with Lavinia in the morning, it seems hardly worthwhile repairing to Mount Street."

"You are making rather free in your sister-in-law's household, my lord," Aurora said, inwardly dismayed at the prospect of the earl's staying in Berkeley Square for the night—or what was left of it.

"Oh, James has his room here, and his things," Lord Albert informed her. "When Will was dying, James spent all his time nursing him, and afterward, with Lavinia prostrated and everything at sixes and sevens, with the servants not knowing what to do and Will's papers having to be gone through, James stayed here for almost two months. Later, he dropped in from time to time to see that the children were properly looked after and such—until Lavinia had recovered and Will's business affairs were settled." He regarded the earl with some concern. "You do look a trifle pale. Are you at all the thing? What I mean is, Roxton Hall isn't—"

"I was up at Oxford executing a favor for a friend. I had just returned to the Hall when I received the intelligence that"—his lips tightened—"that things were not as they should be in Berkeley Square."

"I wonder who dared to run to you with such falsehoods. I would make Lavinia turn him or her out at once. So you started out for London right away?"

The earl nodded, then flung himself into an armchair, stretching out his long legs. "I only allowed myself time to change horses."

"No wonder you're worn out. You must have been on the road for several hours."

"Oh, that," the earl said carelessly. "That is nothing. But I scarcly slept for three days. I was settling old Wychecoombe's affairs, if you must know; and those females of his household! God preserve me from those hysterical creatures. Three of them, not counting the old aunt. And all three of them having vapors at the same time. I felt as if I had landed in Bedlam."

The viscount shuddered. "I should rather think so."

There was a discreet cough. The butler had entered so silently that none of them had heard him. "You rang, my lord?"

"Make my chamber ready, and fetch us some Madeira and"—he glanced at Aurora—"three glasses."

"No, thank you," said Aurora, getting up. "I shall retire to my room now."

The servant bowed and withdrew.

The viscount suddenly remembered his grievance. "You will not—you will not persecute Miss Marshingham for having gone to the masquerade?"

"If she wants to stay under this roof," the earl said wearily, "my brother's house—I hope in the future she will conduct herself with decorum. And that excludes going to opera house masquerades or having Style pay call on her here. As for the rest"—he shrugged—"I would have preferred that she not come here to stay, but if I ask her to leave now, Lavinia will doubtless suffer a near-fatal attack. . . ."

"I think you are being very unfair to Miss Marshingham. When you are better acquainted with her, you will realize how mistaken you have been and you will beg her pardon."

"Don't waste your breath, Lord Deberough," Aurora interjected. "In his lordship's eyes I am beneath contempt, but I shan't lose any sleep over it. Good night, my lords." And sketching them a deep curtsy, she swept out of the room.

- 5 -

SLOWLY AURORA WENT up the wide staircase to her chamber. If the earl's wrath seemed to have abated, hers had also. Not that her outrage at his insulting manners had diminished, but her blood cooled enough for her to consider other things besides her own wounded dignity.

Aurora was not versed in town ways, but she was no fool. It seemed that Lady Clara, who was apparently a bit older than the viscount, had been trying, with the help of the Baron of Style, to entrap Lord Albert into marrying her. As Lord Roxton's heir, the young man was quite a catch. Naturally the earl was concerned about his only surviving brother contracting a good alliance. And that ruled out marriage to a penniless girl such as herself. Moreover, marriage to a girl who seemed to be on intimate terms with a man whom Lord Roxton held in such contempt was unthinkable. It spoke volumes for his concern for his brother that the earl did not even wait to rest at his country estate, but posted at once to London to rescue the viscount from the clutches of a designing female. Aurora only wondered who had acted as a spy and bore tales—exaggerated ones at that—to his lordship. She would ask Lavinia tomorrow.

Young Albert seemed to be fond of his stern brother,

their differences notwithstanding, and concerned for his welfare. But he had no marriage in mind yet, thought Aurora with some relief. If only she could contrive to cool his ardor, she might have no trouble on that head. And then the earl might leave her alone.

Aurora heaved a sigh. She had been in London a few weeks, and she had done practically nothing about finding a suitable position. She could not trespass on Lavinia's hospitality for long, and the earl's appearance on the scene made the matter of her finding a place all the more urgent. To reside in a house where the earl could come and go as he pleased did not suit her at all. She had not the smallest desire to expose herself to his snubs. Nor would she want to cause a brawl in Lavinia's household, which was bound to happen when her own temper got the better of her.

She was opening the door of her bedchamber when she heard her name being called softly. She turned around. Lady Lanville, in a diaphanous lilac dressing gown, her cap askew on her blond curls, was beckoning her to come forward.

Aurora stifled an exclamation of annoyance but trod toward the widow. "Yes?" she asked, somewhat ungraciously.

Lavinia grabbed her by the arm, pulled her into her room, and shut the door.

"Oh, pray tell me what did he say; don't keep me on tenterhooks," Lavinia moaned, raising the vinaigrette to her nostrils. "Did you betray me, Aurora? Oh, don't say you did. I fear my palpitations are getting worse." She sank upon her bed. "You promised, *you promised* you would *not* tell him that I was at that stupid masquerade with Alphonsus," she wailed.

"Calm yourself," Aurora said, eyeing her cousin with some impatience. "I did not say anything that would reveal your part in this affair. The only thing he holds against you is inviting me to stay in your home."

"Oh, thank you, thank you, Aurora. Oh, I am so much obliged to you," cried the widow. "Oh, I knew you would help me in this fix. Was he *dreadfully* angry?"

"He was, but it doesn't signify." A troubled Aurora sat down on a chair beside the bed. "Lavinia, he has a strange notion that I want to entrap Lord Albert into marriage. Who could have given him such information? One of your servants?"

"No, no. They couldn't have. Besides, there's not a grain of truth in it." Abruptly her eyes dilated. "Clara! Of course. Clara . . . She doesn't like it above half that Albert no longer pays court to her. She would be spiteful enough—"

"But Lord Roxton hates her. Wouldn't he think—"

"No, no. She probably contrived to send him a message without divulging her part in the matter. It would be so like her. Odious, scheming woman. Of course she knew Roxton would—"

"But how would Lady Clara know about me?"

Lavinia looked embarrassed.

"Oh, I see," Aurora exclaimed. "You have discussed me with Baron Style, and he is her friend. I will thank you in the future not to discuss me with your friends behind my back."

"But—but I didn't say anything exceptional. Only that you are a very pretty girl and Albert seemed to be quite smitten with you."

"And that was enough for Lady Clara, I collect. And since Lord Albert apparently has stopped paying attention to her, she put two and two together. But why should Lord Roxton think that Lord Style had been helping Lady Clara to entrap Lord Albert into marriage? Is there any truth in it?"

Lady Lanville gave an impatient shake of her head. "Oh, Clara would like to get her hooks into Albert, but that's neither here nor there. I must say, if I had known how things would turn out, I would never have mentioned this to Alphonsus." She sounded affronted. "Not that she wouldn't have discovered how matters stood with Albert in any case."

"Well, it is all to no purpose now," Aurora said somewhat tartly. "What makes the situation awkward is that I am bound to meet Lord Roxton quite often, it seems, and I don't see how I can do so and treat him with civility after the things he has said to me. Tomorrow morning cannot be helped. I wonder if he means to breakfast here."

"Breakfast here? Whatever do you mean?"

"He is staying here for the night."

Lady Lanville's hands flew to her heart. "No!"

"Yes. He gave orders to prepare his bedchamber. I own I am surprised at this arrangement—"

"Oh, that all comes from his staying here after Will— after my husband passed away. I was prostrated, and the nurse was taken ill and the governess had left again, and nobody could quiet the children but him and— Well, I was rather glad to have a man under my roof in those days, and the children like when he comes, Tom especially. Oh, it became an understanding that he treat this house as his own. But afterward, when I recovered, he came to stay very infrequently. But that's beside the point."

She began to wring her hands. "Oh, what shall I do? How shall I contrive to meet Alphonsus now? And if I don't, he might come calling here and that would be fatal. Just *fatal!* I could send a note round to his lodgings, only he mentioned he wouldn't be going home. Something about a card party at a friend's. He was disappointed that our evening was ruined, you see. Oh, was there anything more provoking! That horrible Roxton. Depend upon it, he means to take me to task again tomorrow. And he knows how delicate my constitution is."

Aurora tried to stem this impassioned speech. "Indeed, I fear you are right. I seem to recall his mentioning the need to have a word with you in the morning. But pray enlighten me, Lavinia. What is it all about . . . your meeting Alphonsus, I mean, and why—"

"Oh, it is the most wretched business. I shouldn't have given in. It was quite imprudent of me, but Alphonsus insisted."

"Insisted on what?"

"On meeting him in the park. In a secluded spot. I would go driving in the park and—and then decide to take a stroll and—and Alphonsus would be waiting—"

"You had intended to meet him before breakfast?"

"Yes, for I couldn't do it after breakfast. I'm to be measured for that new dress, and Lady Sauville is calling for me later. Something must be done to avert a *calamity*. Alphonsus must be warned not to come to Berkeley Square unless I send word to him."

"I should have supposed he would have sense enough not to do so when Lord Roxton is in town," Aurora suggested.

"Oh, Alphonsus sometimes seems bent on goading Roxton. But it is perfectly safe for him to visit me at certain times, for usually once Roxton gives me one of his scolds, he removes to Mount Street and doesn't show his face here again until he is persuaded I have recovered completely from the spasms his sermon had inflicted upon me. But what's to be done now? If I don't show up—"

"He will think Lord Roxton has prevented you," Aurora said helpfully.

For a moment Lady Lanville looked hopeful. "I shall write a note this instant. But he might not receive the note in time."

"Send a note tomorrow to the park." Aurora was ready to be done with the matter.

Lavinia pondered that for a moment, then said with regret, "No, it won't answer, for I can't send just anybody."

"What about Bellman? Surely as your personal maid and dresser she can be trusted with such an errand. And she, I am sure, won't be terrified into betraying you. A hatchet-faced female if ever I saw one."

"So she is. And odiously overbearing. But she does wonders with my hair, and she knows all about my clothes and—"

"Well, why not send her?" Aurora asked.

Lady Lanville shook her head categorically. "No, no, no. You don't understand. She is very prim and proper. She would never meet a gentleman clandestinely in the park."

"In that case, the simplest solution of all is to give up the baron." Aurora was getting heartily sick of Lady Lanville's misfortunes.

"What!" shrieked the widow. "You cannot mean that. To give up my only friend, the only one who can contrive to brighten up my widowhood! The only one who understands that I'm too young to sit back and play a staid dowager!"

"Well, you do what you like, I'm off to bed," Aurora said, yawning.

Lavinia jumped off her bed and grasped Aurora by the arm. "But you can't. You can't leave me in this fix. *You* must help me."

"Oh, no!" Aurora put up her hands as if to ward off any further entreaties. "Oh, no! Out of the question—if you mean to send me to meet the baron."

"But you must. No one will think it strange if *you* don't show up for breakfast."

"No! I may not have been on the town, but I do know that a lady is not supposed to venture out on the streets alone, especially walking in the park."

Lavinia stamped her foot. "Oh, what can it signify to you? *Your* aspirations don't go any higher than to obtain a suitable position. It can do no harm for you to go about unattended. No one worries overmuch how *you* go on."

"What if I meet somebody in the park who recognizes me? Some of your acquaintances."

"I am certain you won't. Not at that early hour. And you can wear a cloak and a large bonnet to shade your face. The—the place where I was to meet Alphonsus is secluded. I will give you directions."

"No, I won't do it," Aurora said firmly.

"But you must! Oh, I feel a spasm coming on! Where is my vinaigrette?" Lavinia moaned and fell back on the bed, feebly groping for her smelling salts. "If you don't go, all is at end with me! Roxton will discover that I was to meet Alphonsus, and he will pack me off to Roxton Hall, and I shall die there. I'll just *die!* And Alphonsus would never dare to come visit me at the Hall. Oh, pray ring for my maid. I am going to be dreadfully ill. Oh—and having him discover about Alphonsus on top of that horrid bill."

"Bill—what bill?" Aurora was getting dizzy.

"For my hat," she wailed. "How was I supposed to know it would be so dreadfully expensive? And I looked quite ravishing in it."

Aurora was beginning to feel sympathy for the earl. "Have done, have done! I suppose I shall have to go to this clandestine tryst in your stead. But I wish that you'd picked someone else for your friend, somebody whom Lord Roxton would dislike less than Baron Style."

"But I have known Alphonsus all my life," moaned the

widow. "I knew him even before I met Will. We were even betrothed once."

"What?" Aurora's blue eyes widened in surprise.

"Yes." Abruptly the widow lost her feeble voice. "Oh, I *knew* I could depend on you. You will go, won't you?"

"Yes, I will," Aurora said reluctantly. "After all, it shan't take me above half an hour to discharge my errand. You had better write him a billet."

"Oh, I will, I will. But you must also explain how it is." The widow seemed to have recovered miraculously.

"Lavinia," Aurora suddenly asked, "why does Lord Roxton object to Baron Style so strongly? After all, if he is your friend of such a long standing—"

"Because Roxton is a horrid, unreasonable man. Alphonsus was Will's particular friend too. In fact, they spent the last night before Will's accident playing cards at Style Lodge. But Roxton has never liked Alphonsus. Because he is a gamester, he says. Yet Roxton frequents the gaming hells himself; and it is perfectly all right for him to do so. But when Will would go there with Alphonsus, he would kick up such a dust. Oh, there is no bearing that man!"

Aurora, however, could not believe that was quite the whole explanation for Lord Roxton's aversion to Baron Style. She heaved a sigh. She hated to be embroiled in Lavinia's schemes, but if she didn't it might indeed precipitate a crisis. It seemed also not so difficult after all—to carry a message to the baron from Lavinia. She wouldn't even bother with a carriage. She would walk. A brisk walk would do her good. No need to take anyone with her either, she reflected. Lavinia was right. She, Aurora, was of no consequence to the *ton* whatever. And the sooner she stopped moving in polite circles, the better it would be for her peace of mind.

With a heavy heart and a firm resolve to start looking for a post the following day, Aurora finally retired to her chamber and to bed.

She slept only fitfully, and awoke tired and with a headache that made her cross and quite disinclined to fulfill her promise to Lavinia. But she knew she would carry it out just the same.

She rose, washed briskly in cold water, dressed hastily

in her blue silk walking dress, and, after running a brush
through her auburn locks and putting on a blue bonnet and
a pale-blue cloak, she let herself out of the house.

Only the servants were up and about so early. If they
noticed Miss Marshingham going out alone and at such an
hour, they knew better than to comment upon it. Aurora,
although not at all high in the instep, knew to a nicety how
to depress an impertinent domestic. In fact, the servants
showed more respect to Aurora than they did to their own
mistress.

She walked rapidly along, but even this early she had
to endure several quizzical stares. She paid no heed; they
were of no consequence. But once in the park she had to
be more circumspect. She encountered at least two of Lady
Lanville's male acquaintances exercising their horses, and
she studiously kept her face averted, not wanting them to
recognize her. At last she rounded a corner and arrived at
the appointed place, somewhat breathless but determined
to discharge her errand with all possible speed.

Lord Style was already there, strutting about, a bamboo
walking stick in his hand. He had done justice to the occasion, for he was decked out in the palest of yellow pantaloons, and his olive-green coat must have required the
help of at least two servants to coax him into it. But nothing
could disguise the signs of dissipation on his face, nor his
inclination to stoutness. And in spite of all his finery, or
perhaps because of it, he appeared to Aurora a slightly
ridiculous figure.

He spotted her coming and his eyes widened, but he
doffed his hat with a flourish and executed a deep bow.
Thereupon he took her hand and carried it to his lips. "What
a charming surprise, Miss Marshingham. I am delighted to
see you, and none the worse for last night's adventure. But
pray do tell me, where is Lady Lanville? Not indisposed,
I trust?"

Again that unctuous voice full of blandishment struck
unpleasantly at Aurora's ears. "Lady Lanville was prevented
from coming, for Lord Roxton stayed over at Berkeley
Square and—"

"Ah! That is a pity. That would make it somewhat awk-

ward for her to keep our rendezvous. I trust you both did
not suffer too much at his hands because of last night."

Aurora shrugged. "His temper means nothing to me, but
it upset Lady Lanville."

"Is he—is he aware of the true state of affairs?"

"No, he is not," snapped Aurora. "And I wish you two
would not involve me in your escapades. Here"—she removed from her reticule Lavinia's billet and thrust it in his
hand—"here is Lady Lanville's message to you. She regrets
she won't be able to see you, and she charged me particularly
to beg you not to call on her today. I daresay she'll contrive
to let you know when it would be prudent for you to visit
in Berkeley Square. Though it would be much better were
you not to see her again," she added darkly. "Apparently
Lord Roxton has the uncanny knack of finding out things
one particularly wishes him not to know."

"Yes, he has that ability," agreed Lord Style. He perused
Lady Lanville's missive, then slipped it into his pocket.
"I am desolated, but it cannot be helped. Convey to her
ladyship my deep regret and my most fervent hope that we
shall meet again soon."

"Certainly, I shall do so," Aurora answered with civility.
"And now, having discharged my errand, I must bid you
good-bye, my lord."

"What? So soon? That is a thousand pities. It is such a
fine morning, perfect for a walk in the park—if you allow
me to accompany you. For no lady should walk about unattended." He made as if to take her arm.

Aurora stepped back. "I am perfectly well aware that no
lady should walk alone. You may take a walk in the park,
if you choose, but I must hurry back."

"Allow me then to accompany you home. If not to the
doorstep," he added with a comical expression on his face,
"at least to the square."

"I am very much obliged to you, but pray do not give
yourself the trouble. I can get back very well alone."

She started to walk away.

He placed a restraining hand on her arm. "Ah, but do
not desert me so soon, Miss Marshingham. I have not yet
properly thanked you for coming to my and Lady Lanville's

rescue last night. And today also. You are a very generous woman."

"Much obliged, I'm sure," said Aurora. "But you'd best thank me by not detaining me here any longer."

"*So!* I might have known!" An angry voice struck their ears unpleasantly. The baron released her arm.

Lord Roxton, on a magnificent bay mare, came riding up one of the bridle paths.

- 6 -

THE EARL LOOKED even more impressive on horseback than
on foot. Today he was dressed in an elegant bottle-green
coat, breeches, and top boots. A curly-brimmed beaver hat
covered his dark hair. Aurora had always thought Waldo
had looked most dashing on horseback, yet at this moment
her memory of Waldo was a washed-out image compared
with this splendid picture of manhood. But the earl's countenance was hard and impenetrable.

"Not content with last night's escapade, I see you must
follow it up with this clandestine meeting," he continued
in withering accents. "You'd better find yourself some other
lodgings, if you will persist in making yourself the talk of
the town."

Aurora's blue eyes flashed with indignation. "You have
no right to censor me, my lord. As for my making myself
the talk of the town, I went quite unnoticed—up until your
lordship decided to draw attention to me with your ill-con-
ceived remarks."

Which was perfectly true, for several riders and one or
two saunterers had halted to stare at Aurora's flushed
cheeks, and Baron Style's discomfiture, and at Lord Roxton
astride his horse, looking very stern and forbidding.

"I have every right to protect the good name and reputation of my sister-in-law and my wards," he seethed through his teeth. "As for you"—his brow darkened when he turned to the baron—"I'll thank you not to foist your light skirt upon my brother's household."

Aurora's hands balled into fists. Baron Style drew himself up. "How dare you insult a well-born lady, one who is in some way related to you!"

"She is no relation of mine," said the earl in a contemptuous tone.

"And I, my lord, disclaim any relationship with *you!*" Aurora added. "I would be ashamed to own such an overbearing, insolent man as yourself," she parried, her anger mounting by the second.

Several pairs of eyes now stared at them with unconcealed curiosity.

"For God's sake, James! People are staring," cried the baron.

The earl seemed to suddenly recollect his surroundings. "We shall continue discussing this in Berkeley Square," he said. "What conveyance brought you here?" he demanded of Aurora.

"I walked," she said defiantly.

"You walked," seethed the earl. "And without an abigail to accompany you! It is all of a piece with your character. But then I suppose you would hardly take along a maid to a clandestine tryst."

Aurora, eyes blazing with wrath, did not deign to give him an answer.

"I shall accompany you home," Lord Style proffered boldly.

"You will do no such thing!" thundered the earl. "Stay right here and I shall procure a hackney for— On second thought, *you* procure the carriage, and I shall wait to see Miss Marshingham safely bestowed inside it."

Aurora made him an ironic curtsy. "My lord, you are all solicitude, but your concern is wasted. I can go back very well the way I came. After all, according to Lady Lanville, *my* person is of no consequence to anyone."

The earl frowned and stared at her with an odd expression. But the baron was shocked. "No, no, Miss Marshingham. I am persuaded you must be mistaken. Lady Lanville couldn't have said *that!*"

"Well, there you are wrong," the earl said unexpectedly. "It is exactly the sort of thing she would say. You should know Lavinia well enough to believe that."

Roxton frowned again. "If she is so little concerned for your welfare that she lets you walk about the town unattended, why the devil did she invite you to stay with her?"

Why, so as to have somebody to help her out of her stupid scrapes! Aurora thought angrily.

"Roxton, your language! It is most improper and shocking," began the baron.

The earl, paying him no heed, continued, "Unless it was because she could enjoy you as a companion and a drudge without incurring an expense."

"No, no. You wrong Lavinia." Baron Style defended the widow. "She has a very kind heart."

"Yes, when it doesn't interfere with her welfare and comfort," the earl said scathingly. "Well, don't stand there, Style. Procure a carriage for Miss Marshingham. And don't come back with it, do you hear?"

"My dear fellow, I resent your words and your tone of voice—"

"Resent and be damned. It is no concern of mine."

"Pray, Lord Style, do oblige me by procuring a conveyance for me immediately," said Aurora. "The longer we stay here, the more awkward the situation becomes."

The baron bowed, obviously relieved to escape this embarrassing predicament. "Yes, you are right, of course. I shall do so at once. Pray believe how exceedingly sorry I am to have placed you—"

"Yes, yes, but never mind that. Just go, I beg you." Aurora hastened him on his way. And at last with yet another bow the baron took himself off.

"Never knew a fellow prosing on so," the earl muttered. "What Lavinia could ever see in that bore...However, that's quite beside the point." He broke off abruptly and frowned again. Then he dismounted. "We shall walk until the carriage arrives for you."

Aurora shrugged. "As you wish." There was no point in protesting.

Leading his horse, the earl was still frowning. "Marshingham—Marshingham—I seem to have heard that name before."

"No doubt you have. After all, even if we both deplore the fact, I am Lady Lanville's distant cousin."

The earl waved an impatient hand. "No, no. It was in connection with something else." He rubbed his forehead. "Damnation, the thing escapes me for the moment."

"Pray do not give yourself the trouble of trying to recollect." Aurora said icily. "It is of no matter whatever."

He glared at her. "Oh, yes, you make it abundantly clear to me that my thoughts and my opinions mean nothing to you."

"A *sad* blow to your lordship's consequence, I'm sure. As toadied as you are, it must be a salutary experience for you to meet someone who does not care a whit to stand in your good graces. Aye, that must seem to you quite out of the ordinary."

He raised his heavy brows. "What seems to me more out of the ordinary is how you can abide such a man as Style for your friend."

"I do not—" began Aurora, then broke off. "It is not your lordship's concern."

"But— Oh, devil take it! You are the most exasperating female I have ever met."

"No, really? I thought Lady Lanville, with her swoons and her hysterics, had that distinction."

"Oh, Lavinia. She is a damned nuisance, whereas you—" He glanced at Aurora searchingly. "Does she run you ragged? She can, you know."

Why was this arrogant man so solicitous all of a sudden? What an odd creature he was, thought Aurora. To call her names and then inquire whether she was being treated correctly—almost in the same breath. Her anger was still simmering but now the lid was firmly on her emotions. It was just as well, for to bandy words with his lordship in a public place wouldn't do at all. As it was, she was vexed with herself for allowing herself to be drawn into conversations with him at all. Ignoring him completely would have been more to the purpose and more fitting. Yet there was an arresting quality about this man, an almost palpable force emanating from his person that made it difficult to ignore him.

To her relief he soon lapsed into silence and shortly after, a hackney coach bowled toward them. The driver jumped off and inquired whether she would be the miss he was to drive to Berkeley Square. Aurora nodded and prepared to enter the carriage.

It appeared for a moment as if the earl wanted to hand her up, but while he hesitated, Aurora climbed quickly inside. The earl touched the brim of his hat. "I shall no doubt meet you at Berkeley Square again," he commented. Jumping onto his horse, he whirled round and galloped off, while Aurora's carriage drove off sedately in the opposite direction.

Lavinia pounced on her young cousin as soon as she entered the hall.

"Well, well, did you see Alphonsus?"

Aurora glanced around to ascertain that no servants were eavesdropping. "Yes, I did see him and delivered your message. He sends his regrets. But Lord Roxton came upon me and Lord Style in the park. Now he thinks I am really past praying for."

Lady Lanville shuddered dramatically. "Wasn't it providential that I did not go there!"

Not one thought did she give to Aurora. Aurora's lips curled in an ironic twist. Well, what else could she expect? For a moment the idea flashed through her mind to tell Lord Roxton the truth, but she dismissed it at once as unworthy. She was not one to bear tales or break her word, and she would not try to justify herself before that overbearing man. That would be beneath contempt. But she should inform Lavinia of what the earl had said. "He—Lord Roxton—quite delighted in taking me to task once again."

"Oh, how provoking! I hope he does not call again for days, for he usually doesn't. I shall have to retire to my bedchamber in any case. Oh, it is *most* vexing—for I have so many things to do."

Aurora raised a quizzical eyebrow.

"Oh, but you don't know the whole story. Come, let us

repair to one of the parlors, and I shall tell you all about it."

Reluctantly Aurora allowed herself to be led into the drawing room, while the widow continued. "My friend Lady Silverton sent a note round to me just as I was sitting down to breakfast. Oh, did you have breakfast?" she added belatedly.

Aurora shook her head.

"Well, ring the bell and desire it to be brought up. Where was I? Oh yes. The note from Lady Silverton. I am to expect an invitation to the ball in honor of the grand duchess."

Aurora blinked. "Which grand duchess?"

"Why, the Grand Duchess of Oldenburg, of course. The tsar's sister. There is a ball being held in her honor. Surely you must have heard of it. I shall want a new gown and— What shall you wear?"

Aurora shrugged. "One of my old gowns. But I wasn't aware I was invited."

"But of course you are. You are staying with *me*. It's the least I can do for you." She shook her head. "One of your old gowns? No, no, Aurora. That won't do! To be wearing a secondhand gown to a ball for the grand duchess would be too *shabby*."

"Why? I'm sure she won't care a button."

"No, no. We must have a gown made for you as well."

"I can't afford a new ball gown. And Lord Roxton would certainly object to your spending money on my gown."

Lady Lanville was much struck with this observation. Her smooth brow creased, then cleared. "I know. I shall have two dresses made for myself. He cannot object to *that*. For how can I tell which one would be most becoming to me until I have tried them on."

Aurora could not help being amused by this ingenious scheme. "But your gowns don't fit me precisely."

"Oh, that is just a trifle. It won't take Madame Flandin's seamstress above two hours to fit the gown to your figure, our height being the same. I shall desire one of the gowns to be made a trifle loose fitting. You know, the more I think of it, the better I like it, for indeed I might have a hard time deciding which gown to choose."

"Do as you wish, but don't trouble yourself on my account." Aurora sighed. "In fact, I trust by that time I shall have found a suitable position and no longer be trespassing on your hospitality."

"Nonsense," said the widow pettishly. "I am surprised you persist in that ridiculous notion. What you ought to do is achieve a respectable alliance. London is full of eligible bachelors."

"And just as full of debutantes and matchmaking mamas. No, thank you. I won't compete with them." Aurora bristled.

"You have no need to compete with them, for you're no simpering miss. You, Aurora, have both address and beauty."

"I am much obliged to you." Aurora smiled. "I know I am not precisely an antidote, but what eligible bachelor would consider a girl practically on the shelf and penniless to boot?"

Penniless . . . If she hadn't been penniless, Waldo would have married her—and that, she now realized, would have been a tragic mistake.

"I am persuaded there must be scores of bachelors who are not hanging out for a rich wife; and so you shall discover when I take you to Almack's." Lavinia looked delighted with herself.

"What? Are you actually going to bring me within the hallowed precincts of the marriage mart?"

"You shouldn't scorn Almack's. It *is* the best place for a lady to meet a gentleman and vice versa. And why not? After all, people *do* have to become acquainted somewhere, don't they? I was thinking you should have a new dress."

"Pray do not go to all that trouble, I beg you. I—"

"But don't you understand? To be allowed to attend Almack's assemblies is the greatest honor. Not everyone is so lucky as to have that privilege."

"No need to explain to me," said Aurora, nettled. "We in Yorkshire are not such clodpoles as not to know that having an entrée to Almack's is almost the greatest social distinction one can receive. Indeed, in my salad days it was my greatest ambition to attend one of the assemblies."

"Salad days—no, indeed, Aurora. And you only three and twenty. I see it is more imperative than ever for you to attend Almack's. And in a new gown too."

"But how could you procure a voucher for me?" Aurora asked.

"Oh, that is easily done. I know several of the patronesses. Where were we? Oh, yes—a new gown for you to wear to Almack's. Do you know, I believe I still have that powder-blue silk. I believe if I asked Bellman she could find it for me. It would make a splendid gown for you."

"I am much obliged to you, but somebody will still have to sew the gown and—" It seemed to Aurora that her financial problems loomed around every twist of the conversation.

"Oh, don't worry about that expenditure. Once you are creditably established—"

"Creditably established! I think you have windmills in your head! You'd best forget all about my attending Almack's. It just won't do. Suppose I were to meet the parents of my future charges?"

"But I must take you to Almack's. I promised Aunt Martha I would. *Oooh—*"

Aurora's blue eyes flashed with anger. "So! You and Aunt Martha have hatched this scheme between you. Well, I shall thank you both for taking such an interest in my affairs."

"Indeed, you *should*. For nothing would please me and Aunt Martha more than to see you make a brilliant match. She has your welfare at heart, and so have I. And poor Aunt Martha and Uncle Horace are pretty hard up, having you three on their hands. It would be a load off her mind to see you married to an eligible gentleman."

Aurora bit her lip. "I am well aware that we have been and still are a great charge on Uncle Horace and Aunt Martha. That is why I am seeking a post, and as soon as I can earn some money, I shall send for my sisters." How maddening not to be independent!

"Fiddlesticks. Those arrangements just won't do at all. You had better think how to catch a rich husband."

Aurora sighed. It was useless to persuade Lady Lanville to her own thinking. Lavinia would never understand that trying to catch a husband seemed to Aurora excessively vulgar. Besides, she had no intention of marrying without love. In spite of her bitter romantic disappointment, she harbored an image of marriage with deep affection on both sides. That possibility seemed very remote for her now.

"Was Lord Roxton—was he very much vexed with you?" Lavinia asked, changing the subject.

"Vexed isn't the word for it. He—he has the devil's own temper."

"There. What did I tell you!" the widow said with satisfaction. "You had better contrive to fall into a swoon or have spasms. Nothing so puts him off as a hysterical female. He shall leave you alone if you do that."

Aurora smiled fondly at her cousin. "Is that what you are doing—pretending to be ill?"

Lavinia rolled eyes to the ceiling. "Alas, I have a very delicate constitution. The veriest upset brings on my palpitations. I don't need to pretend. But you—I am persuaded you have never swooned in your life."

"Very likely. I don't remember ever having done so."

"I'm sure I don't know where you have inherited your constitution. But that's neither here nor there. Have your breakfast, then come to my room. I shall show you the blue silk."

Aurora gave an inward sigh. She might as well humor Lavinia by agreeing to her plans and seize this opportunity of attending Almack's, for it probably would her last chance to attend the assemblies. She was strongly tempted to have one final fling, to make one last appearance in the brilliant society in which she would have moved as a matter of course were it not for that careless trustee, that executor of her father's will. Were Papa still alive, things might not have gone so badly with them, for though they were impoverished, they had always managed to keep one step ahead of the creditors. But that odious Sir Boniface Cudsworth had made such a bad job of taking care of what was left of the estate that she and her sisters were forced to sell all the

lands and Treeton Hall just to stay clear of debts. If it
weren't for Aunt Martha and Uncle Horace, they would
have been begging on the streets.

Should she try to catch a rich husband as Lavinia suggested? It would go much against the grain, but for the sake
of her sisters and Aunt Martha she had to do something.
Well, she would attend Almack's and still try to obtain a
suitable post. Let the future show what course she ought to
follow.

· 7 ·

THE MORNING BEFORE they were to attend Almack's, an unexpected caller arrived in Berkeley Square. Lavinia was at a mantua maker's, and Aurora was sitting in the drawing room, trying to compose a letter to Aunt Martha and Priscilla. Stobbins entered the room, gave an apologetic cough, and said, "Pardon me, miss, but there is a young person desiring to see Lady Lanville. A young lady."

Aurora, slightly impatient at having the trend of her thoughts interrupted, said with a shrug, "Lady Lanville is not at home, as you are well aware. You don't need me to tell you how to send her about her business."

"Begging your pardon, miss. I think miss ought to see this one."

"But she hasn't come to see me and I am persuaded—" Then, seeing the butler's embarrassed but obstinate expression, she said, "Well, what is it? Who is she?"

"As to who, I am not able to say. She didn't give her name. But the young lady is hardly out of the schoolroom and—and she is carrying a bandbox and seems very frightened."

Aurora's eyes showed more interest. "A runaway, eh? I wonder who she could be." Thinking of her two motherless

53

sisters, she said, "Desire her to come up. No, on second thought, I shall go down. Thank you, Stobbins. I think you did right in not turning her away."

The butler bowed his acknowledgment, and his ramrod figure straightened to an even loftier stance.

Upon entering the yellow salon, Aurora observed a young damsel of about seventeen years of age, attired in a gown of sprig muslin and a pink pelisse, sitting on the edge of the settee and nervously twisting her fingers. A small band-box stood on the floor at her feet and beside it a pair of pink gloves, which had apparently slipped from her hands. The girl was small and slender, with tiny hands and feet, like a china figurine. Her light-brown ringlets were bound with a pink ribbon, and a pink hat rested on the settee at her side.

The girl started at Aurora's entrance. She jumped to her feet, and her enormous green eyes stared at her hostess in a pathetic expression of entreaty and apprehension. The perfect rosebud mouth trembled.

Aurora stepped closer. "I am Aurora Marshingham," she said, giving the girl a friendly smile. "Lady Lanville is from home, but I shall be happy to be of service to you in her stead."

"Oh, pray, if you only *could!* Are you staying with Lady Lanville? Do you know my brother?" She spoke in a pleasant voice, which seemed to quaver with fear.

Aurora grasped the cold hands in her own and pressed them reassuringly. "As I do not know your name, I cannot be perfectly sure if I know—"

The girl became even more flustered. "Oh, what am I about! Only—only I was afraid to give my name to the butler for fear he would turn me away. I know my brother is not looked on with favor by anybody here except Lady Lanville. But she is his particular friend, and I was per-suaded that she would be so obliging as to help me. For I do not know who to turn to in this fix."

Aurora sat down beside her on the settee. "I'm sure Lady Lanville would be only too glad to help you," she said, being not at all sure. "But don't you think one's own brother would be the best person to help one in a fix?"

Pressing her hands to her heaving bosom, the frightened girl cried, "Oh, no, no! He wouldn't. He mustn't even *know* that I am here. He would be excessively angry. You see, Alfie has favored this match and—"

Aurora knit her brows. "Are you by any chance the sister of Baron Style?"

The damsel blinked in confusion. "Didn't I say so? I beg your pardon. Pray forgive me for being so witless. Yes, I am Melanie Fant, and I am actually his half sister. My mama was Alfie's stepmother, only she didn't live very long after I was born. And Alfie—he hates my calling him that, but I do so, for when I was little I could not pronounce Alphonsus, such a mouthful—Alfie is badly in need of money, on account of his gaming, you see, and because he would like to buy back the estates...."

This time it was Aurora who blinked. "Estates? I'm not sure I understand."

"Oh. Perhaps I ought not to have spoken about it. But everybody knows that. I mean, Alphonsus has been trying to buy back those lands for ages and so did Papa. Of course Papa had no feather to fly with most of the time either." Seeing that Aurora still looked puzzled, Melanie explained. "Grandpapa, or was it Great-Grandpa, I'm not perfectly sure, lost most of the family lands by gaming, and Papa and Alphonsus have been trying to get them back. Only Lord Roxton wouldn't sell."

"Oh," said Aurora, beginning to understand. Perhaps this pink confection could shed some light on the animosity between Roxton and Style.

"Yes, well, Alfie hasn't quite given up hope of getting the estates back—if only he could scrape together enough money." She paused to take a breath.

"But how is it I haven't heard about you?" Aurora exclaimed.

"Oh, that is nothing to be wondered at, for I have been in boarding schools ever since Papa's death. Alfie couldn't be—I mean, what gentleman would like to be saddled with a child to take care of? Of course he was vexed at having to provide for me when he himself is so shockingly expensive. You see, he dresses in the first stare of fashion," she said with simple pride. Then she blushed. "But you must know that, being acquainted with my half brother. You are, are you not?"

Aurora nodded. "Yes, I am, slightly. Through Lady Lanville."

"Then you cannot wonder that he—he could hardly own me, could he? A Pink of the *ton*—and I was just a small brat with spots."

"You don't have any spots now. You are a lady."

"Yes, so Alfie said the last time he came to visit me at the boarding school. That's when he got it into his head to marry me off to his friend Lord Burgley. It so happens that he—that is, Lord Burgley—is looking for a wife, and he is odiously wealthy. Only—only I couldn't. I just couldn't! He is old. Quite old. Even older than Alfie. He must be at least sixty, besides being quite stout and bald. I could never marry him, *never!* Not even to oblige Alfie. Perhaps if I didn't have the image of *another* in my heart . . ." She broke off, pressing her hands to her mouth. The large green eyes filled with tears.

"How could I marry Lord Burgley when I love *him!*" she added. "Even though I know it is quite hopeless."

Aurora was both touched and amused by the girl's confidences. She seemed to be as trusting as a kitten. And just as helpless. "Of course marriage with Lord Burgley is not to be thought of," she agreed wholeheartedly. "But perhaps you ought not to consider your love as hopeless. Is the young man—I gather he is young and handsome?"

"Oh, yes," breathed Melanie, her eyes lighting up.

"Is he someone whom your brother would not quite approve of, perhaps?"

"Oh, no. He is of very good birth and will inherit a large fortune and a title, but—but—" She reddened. "He isn't even aware of my existence."

Aurora raised her brows.

"Well, you—you see, I have been in love with him for years and years, ever since I saw him paying a call on my brother. Well, he wasn't paying a call exactly. His elder brother was. I was on vacation at the manor at that time. Oh, he was so handsome then, such lovely curly hair and these blue eyes of his. But of course he didn't pay any attention to me. And that is not to be wondered at. I was a positive antidote in those days. I haven't met him since, though I have dreamed of him often. And then—I saw him again, years later—at the races. He was a man then but I would have recognized him anytime. And he was even more handsome than as a boy. I had coaxed a girl at the school whose Papa owns racing horses into taking me along. And I saw *him*."

"And did he see you?" Aurora asked.

"Oh, no. At least if he did, he took no notice of me. I was wearing a perfectly dowdy dress and Diana, the girl I was with, is so beautiful, nobody would look twice at me in her presence."

"But if he is such an eligible young man, why don't you ask your brother to arrange a meeting?"

The girl colored even more. "Oh, no! I could never divulge *his* name to Alfie. Never! And you must promise— I beg you, promise me not to divulge my confidences to Alfie." She was becoming quite agitated and had started wringing her hands again.

"Do not distress yourself, Melanie," said Aurora. "If I may call you that?" The curly head nodded. "Of course I shall not betray your confidences, but I do not see why telling your brother—"

"No, no, you do not understand! *His* family would never approve of me. At least Lord R— At least the person who signifies most wouldn't. Besides, I am penniless. I am not a good match for him and he—he doesn't care a button for me, so how could I—"

A discreet knock interrupted this outpouring. Melanie started like a frightened hare. "Oh, I pray it isn't Lord Roxton. If he were to find me here—"

But it was only Stobbins. "The Viscount Deberough begs leave to see you, miss," he said in a disapproving tone.

Aurora thought rapidly. "Desire him to come here, Stobbins." As the butler hesitated, casting a meaningful glance in Melanie's direction, she assured him somewhat impatiently, "It is perfectly all right. In fact, I may require his lordship's assistance."

The butler bowed and withdrew.

The young viscount, impeccably attired in pale-yellow pantaloons and a olive-green coat, entered the room. He stopped on the threshold, perceiving that Aurora was not alone. But it was Melanie's reaction that Aurora was observing. For upon hearing the viscount's name, the girl had uttered a light exclamation, half rose, then sank back, her countenance going white, then red again, her hand flying to her palpitating bosom. Now as she gazed at him, her enormous green eyes grew even larger, and the rosebud mouth opened in wonder and excitement.

Aurora believed she had solved the puzzle. And she understood Melanie's reluctance to disclose the identity of the object of her passion. That connection the earl would tolerate even less than Lady Lanville's friendship with Melanie's brother.

"I beg pardon, ma'am, I was not informed you had company. If you desire me to leave—" Albert hesitated.

"On the contrary, I want to present you to the young lady. But do take a good look at her. Do you recollect ever seeing her before?"

The viscount approached the settee and bowed deeply over Aurora's hand. Then his eyes fastened on the damsel in his first good look. His brows knitted. "It is odd. I have the feeling of having seen you somewhere, ma'am. And yet I could not possibly have done so—for I could never have forgotten so lovely a countenance as yours."

Aurora's eyes danced with mischief. She had thought of Lord Albert for Priscilla but it would have been almost impossible to accomplish such a match. So why not let young Albert transfer his affections from herself to this lovely girl, who obviously thought him a demigod? Aurora could thus help this poor lonely waif and in doing so rid herself of an unwelcome admirer. Even better, she would thrust a spoke in the earl's wheel—for Melanie, in his eyes, would be even more ineligible than herself as a sister-in-law.

Melanie's lips formed a soundless "oh." But Aurora said, performing the introductions, "You have met her, at least on two occasions. My lord Deberough—Miss Melanie Fant, Baron of Style's sister."

The viscount's eyes widened. "What? Not the little freckle-faced brat that was used to be such an infernal nuisance when Will and I visited Style Manor?" He recollected himself immediately. "Miss Fant, I ought not to have spoken those words." He shook his head. "You have grown into a prodigious beauty. I wonder Alphonsus don't bring you out." He bowed low over her hand.

The adoring eyes lifted to his face. "He—Alphonsus—wants me to marry Lord Burgley," the girl said tragically. "So I have run away to cast myself on the mercy of Lady Lanville."

A thunderous look crept over the viscount. "What? To give such a delicate young flower to *that* old roué? The thought is not to be borne! Alphonsus must have taken leave of his senses to suggest such a thing."

"But you see, Lord Burgley is so very rich, and he wouldn't mind my being penniless."

"Oh, wouldn't he? Of course he wouldn't. Alphonsus is a cad to arrange such an alliance. I do beg your pardon, but I cannot hear of such a match." He took an impatient turn about the room.

"No person of sensibility could," Aurora agreed. "That is why we must devise a plan to save Miss Fant from such a horrid fate. Miss Fant relies upon the good will of Lady Lanville, and I'm sure her ladyship would help her gladly were she not so taken up with preparing herself for the two balls. I am persuaded she would have little time to spare for Miss Fant's troubles. So why don't we put our heads together and think up a suitable solution to this problem?" Aurora was enjoying herself thoroughly.

Melanie Fant clasped her hands prayerfully. "Oh, that is *so* kind of you, Miss Marshingham. But perhaps his lordship wouldn't care—"

"Of course I should care." Lord Albert's blue eyes showed great warmth. "That is so like you, Miss Marshingham, to think of others rather than yourself, for I am persuaded you will incur Lavinia's displeasure over this. Of course we must help Miss Fant. But how?"

"First, we must prevail upon Lady Lanville to keep Melanie here for a while and take her out into society."

"An excellent suggestion," approved the viscount. His

brow clouded. "But she would be bound to meet that old rogue Burgley. He is received everywhere."

"Yes, but if you were to accompany us, my lord, I am persuaded you could contrive to keep him at arm's distance from Miss Fant."

The viscount's eyes lighted up. "By Jove, you are right, Miss Marshingham. Of course I could do that easily."

"The only fly in the ointment would be Lord Roxton. I am afraid he would not quite like the scheme." Aurora gestured hopelessly.

"Oh, the devil fly away with James. He doesn't like anything I do. But he cannot possibly object to Miss Fant. She is not responsible for Alphonsus's actions. Besides, at the time of Will's death I am persuaded she must have been still sewing samplers in the schoolroom."

Aurora pricked up her ears. "At the time of Will's death." That phrase must hold a key to Roxton's dislike of the Baron of Style, she decided. She knew that on the night of the accident Lavinia's husband and Lord Style were together gambling and drinking. Was there more to it? Did Baron Style resent Lord Lanville because he had married the woman Style desired? It seemed impossible that the flighty megrim-ridden widow could inspire such passion in any man's breast. But then there was not accounting for taste. She said evenly, "I am persuaded Lord Roxton could be brought to realize that Miss Fant should be an object of his solicitude rather than his anger. It is my hand in the affair that he shall object to."

Melanie's large eyes were blinking from one to the other. "Oh, pray do not . . . I wouldn't for the world trouble . . . I beg you will not put yourself to—"

"I have it," the viscount suddenly cried slapping himself on the knee. "We shall tell James *I* have thought of the plan of keeping Miss Fant here and of bringing her out. He might not quite like it, but once he has seen her, I am sure he will not have the least objection. And his wrath won't fall on your head, Miss Marshingham."

Aurora could see that Albert was already much struck by the helpless beauty of Lord Style's sister.

"I say," the viscount continued, "I have another splendid thought. By allowing us to keep Miss Fant here and pre-

venting her from marrying Burgley, James would be spiking
Alphonsus's guns. That might reconcile him to our plan."

"Yes, oh, yes. I am sure you are right on that score,"
agreed Aurora. "Only—" Lord Roxton could hardly fail to
see the attraction between the two young people. However,
she was not going to let that consideration stand in the way.
"I wonder if Lord Style would try to remove his sister from
us by force," she worried aloud.

Melanie blanched and shrank back, but the viscount said
with assurance, "He would not dare remove her from this
house. He is forbidden entry here. But it's true, she is a
minor, I collect, and he might try removing her when—No,
no, he would hardly create a brawl at Almack's."

"But as the child's brother he might simply step up to
us and claim her," Aurora pointed out. "In the eyes of the
world we have no right to stay him. After all, he is probably
her guardian too. I own I had not thought of that when I
put forward the notion of us bringing her into society."

"Is he your guardian?" asked the viscount of the girl.

Melanie nodded unhappily.

"Then we must keep her here," Aurora decided. "It will
be dull for her, being unable to go out, but it will be better
than risking being torn from our side. And I am persuaded
the servants will not divulge her presence here."

"Oh, they will not, and even perhaps James won't. But
what of Lavinia?" asked Lord Albert glumly. "We are bound
to have some pretty goings-on. Not that I'm not up to it to
handle the situation," he added manfully.

"Oh, pray, Lord Deberough, I beg you, do not put yourself out. I won't— Oh," Melanie cried, swayed, and would
have fallen but for Aurora's protective arm.

The viscount sprang up in alarm. "You are feeling ill.
Shall I fetch a doctor? Bring some hartshorn or Lavinia's
smelling salts?"

"No, no. I beg you. Do not trouble yourself," whispered
Melanie. "It is nothing. Only I had nothing to eat since
yesterday."

"Oh, where have my wits gone abegging?" Aurora cried,
pulling on the bell rope. When a footman appeared, she
commanded, "Bring us some Madeira and cakes or perhaps
a glass of ratafia. Bring all three and desire the cook to

prepare a light meal for our visitor."

The footman's raised brows expressed his astonishment, but he bowed and withdrew.

There was bound to be some gossip in the servants' quarters, thought Aurora, but that didn't signify. She turned back to Melanie, who had recovered somewhat and was sitting starry-eyed and blushing rosily, while the viscount solicitously chafed her hands.

She patted Melanie's arm. "You shall feel more the thing as soon as you have eaten something. And we shall have to procure some clothes for you, for I collect that bandbox doesn't hold much above the barest necessities. We could send for your things, of course, but that might reveal your whereabouts to your brother."

"No. That must not happen. I shall be most happy to procure anything that is required for Miss Fant," offered the viscount. "And if I myself cannot, I shall gladly escort Miss Marshingham to all the shops to make the necessary purchases."

Melanie became flustered again. "Oh, pray, do not. I beg you not to trouble yourself."

Just then a maid entered with a tray of cakes, glasses, and bottles of wine and ratafia. Lord Albert poured out refreshment while Melanie nibbled on a cake. To make Melanie more at ease, as the viscount informed Aurora in an aside, he began to chat to her about unexceptional topics, succeeding so well as to even draw from her a watery chuckle.

Aurora unobtrusively moved farther away from the couple and observed with critical appraisal that they would make a good match. The viscount would not be happy with a strong-willed female or a shrew, and if he really fell in love with this pretty, bird-witted child, she would make him a good wife. She obviously adored him and would do anything to please him. Their marriage would be a convivial one—dull, but convivial.

Aurora's musings were interrupted by an imperious knock on the door, which burst open to reveal Lord Roxton in top boots and breeches, dragging an unwilling and outraged Lavinia into the room.

- 8 -

JAMES, HOW DARE you behave in this peremptory fashion!"
the widow protested loudly as Lord Roxton calmly entered.
"To stride into my parlor without even asking me. Aurora,
Albert, who is this girl? What is she doing here?"

Aurora rose leisurely from her seat, while the two young
people, who had drawn imperceptibly closer, sprang apart
and jumped to their feet. Melanie, pale, was dramatically
pressing her hands to her heaving bosom; Lord Albert took
a manful stance, ready to do battle with his brother and the
world to shield and protect her.

Lord Roxton surveyed the pair with a puzzled frown.

Aurora stepped foward. "Lady Lanville, Lord Roxton,
may I present to you Miss Melanie Fant, who has come to
seek refuge in Berkeley Square."

Melanie gave them a shaky curtsy and a scared glance
out of wide eyes.

Lavinia acknowledged the introduction with an irritated,
absentminded nod. "Charmed, I'm sure."

The earl gave a stiff bow, his brows drawn together.
"Fant? Surely—"

"She is Alphonsus's sister," interposed the viscount.

63

"Half sister," corrected Aurora.

"Well, half sister, that don't signify. The important thing is, Alphonsus wants to marry the girl to old Burgley."

"Oh, he does? And pray what concern is it of yours if he does?" His brother scowled.

"James, do but look at her. You cannot be so heartless as to condemn this child to a marriage with that old reprobate."

"I am not condemning her," said the earl, stripping off his gloves. "Style is."

"But what has all this to do with me?" fretted Lavinia.

"Haven't I just said?" Aurora retorted. "The child came to throw herself on your mercy, to beg you to rescue her from this terrible fate." Before Lavinia could protest further, Aurora hurried on. "She could stay in Berkeley Square until Lord Burgley gives up the notion of marrying her."

"Which he will do soon enough"—the viscount spoke up—"for he's had his eye on one of the Stanton girls these many months. Alphonsus must have persuaded him that his sister would make him a more complaisant wife, but he won't wait overlong for Melanie to show up."

The earl made an ironic bow toward Aurora. "And it is *you*, Miss Marshingham, who I am to thank for this excellent scheme," he said, his gray eyes glittering with frost.

"Oh, I think I *shall* have a spasm!" cried the widow, collapsing onto the nearest sofa and hunting in her reticule for her vinaigrette. "Everybody gives orders in my house except me. I declare I must be the most ill-used creature alive!"

The earl cast her a look of intense annoyance. Lord Albert remained nonplussed, while Melanie, suddenly jolted into action, rushed toward the widow and sank onto her knees beside her. "Oh, no, no, ma'am! Indeed, no! Pray do not . . . I beg you not to distress yourself on my account. I shall go back to Alfie and—and marry Lord Burgley. Only do not . . ." The rest of her speech became unintelligible as it came muffled through her sobs. She grasped Lavinia's hand in her agitation.

Lavinia pressed her other hand to her brow. "Oh, I don't know what this is all coming to. When Alphonsus hears of this—"

"But that's just it," the viscount interrupted. "He mustn't hear of it. You mustn't tell him."

"Not tell Alphonsus!" shrieked the widow. "I couldn't do that!"

"Yes, you could," persisted Lord Albert.

"I am always imposed upon," groaned Lavinia, fortifying herself with a sniff at her vinaigrette.

"Lavinia, don't go off into strong hysterics now. And you, Melanie, stop your bleating," the earl cried with exasperation, hurling his gloves onto a table with a savage thrust. "God preserve me from hysterical females!"

"I must beg you, James," protested the viscount, "to treat Miss Fant with at least a semblance of common civility."

"Now don't you start putting on airs, Albert. I knew Melanie Fant when she was a baby. I even dangled her on my knee, though I daresay she does not remember it. I must own I have forgotten her existence, or rather I thought Alphonsus must have married her off, for he never wanted any part of the brat."

"James!"

"She was an ugly little thing. It's amazing how she has blossomed out. Quite passable now. But not much wit," he added scathingly.

Lord Albert took a menacing step toward his brother. Melanie began to sob even more loudly. And Lady Lanville groaned, "I cannot take care of the child, and I cannot deceive Alphonsus. I just *cannot!*"

Aurora regarded the scene with a twinkle of appreciation. Lord Roxton particularly disliked such spectacles. The earl must have been reading her mind, for he suddenly rounded on her. "So this all amuses you, I collect. It seems to me that this was all *your* contrivance!"

Aurora gave him a polite curtsy. "To be sure, my lord. Everything is always my fault."

"You shall treat Miss Fant with respect, James," Lord Albert declared stoutly, "and you shall give her shelter under your roof, Lavinia, and will not tell Alphonsus anything about her."

But no one paid heed to his words. The earl continued to glare at Aurora, who decided it was time to take control of the situation.

In a few swift strides she was beside Lady Lanville, giving her ladyship a strong shake. "Now, listen to me, Lavinia. You will not have the vapors and you will give this child shelter, and you will not tattle on her to Lord Style. At least not until we have decided what is best to be done about her. Remember, Lavinia," she added meaningfully, "you owe me a favor—two favors, in fact. I demand that you return those favors now. If you don't, you shall find soon enough you'll have greater cause for hysterics."

"I shall never know a moment's—" the widow started, then suddenly she broke off, gulped, and blinked rapidly. "W-what—what do you mean, *greater cause*, Aurora? No, oh, no!"

Out of the corner of one eye, Aurora observed Lord Roxton frowning heavily.

"Pray collect yourself, Lavinia. You must know what I mean."

The widow moaned and sniffed at her vinaigrette, but to the great amazement of both her brothers-in-law, she seemed to have suddenly recovered from her spasms, for she sat up straight on the sofa and regarded Aurora with a hostile yet resigned stare.

"Miss Fant, stop your sobbing this instant," Aurora demanded, "if you do not want to give Lord Roxton a strong dislike of you. That would do nothing to advance your cause." She raised the sobbing girl from the floor. "I will help you all I can, but I shan't be able to do so if you keep on being a watering pot in the presence of his lordship. You must know he hates vapors worst of all."

The two gentlemen watched in fascination as the damsel hiccoughed, gulped, then ceased her sobbing. Aurora handed her her own handkerchief. "Here, dry your eyes, beg everyone's pardon, and sit down here on that sofa. You must excuse her, my lord. Miss Fant has had nothing to eat since last night. Have another cake, Melanie, and your nunchèon will be ready soon. And you, Lord Deberough, pray be so obliging as not to set up Lord Roxton's hackles. Heated words won't answer in this case. Pour Miss Fant another glass of ratafia and pour yourself and his lordship some wine."

Mechanically, as though in a daze, Lord Albert moved

to carry out her orders. The earl regarded Aurora with un-willing respect and approbation. He made her another bow, this time free of irony. "My compliments, Miss Mar-shingham. You are quite a redoubtable person. You have handled them admirably."

"It is hardly an accomplishment, my lord. The possession of two younger sisters and an aunt prone to the vapors has taught me how to handle a situation of this sort. Won't you be seated, my lord. This is a somewhat delicate situation, and naturally your counsel is as appreciated as it is needed."

His dark brows rose quizzically. "An olive branch, Miss Marshingham?"

"Hardly that, my lord. But our quarrel has nothing to do with Miss Fant's predicament. The child wasn't even aware of my existence until she stepped over this threshold."

"She seems to have been aware of my br—of my family's existence," said the earl, frowning.

"It is scarcely surprising since you yourself admitted you knew her; and I understand your family and the family of Baron Style have been well acquainted."

"We have been, more's the pity," the earl said curtly.

Melanie Fant raised her head, looking frightened. It seemed as if at any moment she might burst into tears once more.

"Oh, don't tease yourself," the earl said irritably. "This has nothing to do with you. You were just a child at the time of Will's death."

"Exactly what I thought," approved the viscount. "Me-lanie—Miss Fant—can't be held accountable for her brother's actions."

The earl cast himself into a chair and continued frowning. "I have no desire to oblige Alphonsus by returning you to him or even betraying your presence here," he said, ad-dressing himself to Melanie again. "Nor do I object to your staying in Berkeley Square. But I'm not at all certain Lady Lanville will find herself equal to the task of taking proper care of you."

"I'm afraid you are right, Roxton," moaned the widow, emerging from behind her handkerchief, into which she had been quietly sniffling.

"Oh, do not fret yourself over that, my lady," Aurora

said cheerfully. "I shall make sure she won't be a burden on your nerves."

"Well, in that case, I'm sure *I* have no objection to the chit's staying—if Roxton does not object. But not to tell Alphonsus—"

"Depend upon it, he won't ask you if she is here," said Lord Albert, "for it would never enter his head that she might have come here."

There was an interruption as Stobbins entered, bearing a tray. He bowed. "You desired a nuncheon for the young lady, Miss Marshingham?"

Of course he would come himself. He was dying of curiosity, as were all the help, thought Aurora. "Thank you, Stobbins. You may set it on this table. Perhaps you could ask Mrs. Blight to prepare a room for the young lady. She will be staying here—but no one is to know that. I don't need to tell you how to be discreet, but pray be so obliging as to make sure the rest of the staff shall keep silent about it. Lady Lanville particularly desires it so."

The butler glanced at the earl, whose face remained inscrutable, then toward the widow, who nodded feebly. "Very well," said Stobbins, his face wooden. He bowed politely and withdrew.

The earl leveled his quizzing glass in Aurora's direction. "I must revise some of my earlier opinions of you," he said, studying her with a thoughtful frown. "It is obvious that you were born to command."

Aurora's chin went up. "Naturally, my lord. If it weren't for a series of unfortunate incidents, I would now be the mistress of my own household."

"And you think to become a governess or a schoolteacher," wailed Lavinia. "What will Aunt Martha say."

"Schoolteacher! Governess!" repeated the earl. "Is that your real ambition, Miss Marshingham? I would have thought—"

"My ambition is not at all your concern." Aurora replied, cutting him short. "I shall thank you to remember that."

The earl bared his teeth in a half-amused, half-irritated grin. "So you are still on the warpath."

"After what has passed between us, my lord, we can

hardly be friends ever. However, I don't see why *I* at least cannot behave myself in a civilized manner when the occasion demands it."

The earl gave a loud oath, startling Melanie into spilling some of her ratafia and drawing a reproachful frown from his brother.

"You are the most provoking female of my acquaintance. I only wish I knew what you are really about."

"Just be grateful, my lord, that I don't regale you with a fit of the vapors," said Aurora. "And in any case, I cannot and will not trespass on Lady Lanville's hospitality overlong. As soon as we have settled the problem of Miss Fant, and as soon as the two balls are behind us, I shall set about to remove myself from Berkeley Square."

"Aurora, what can you mean by that?" shrieked the widow. "Never tell me that you've actually found a post?"

"Not yet. But I have put my name down and—"

"Oh, nothing will come of that, I'm sure," Lavinia said, much relieved. "Or if they offer you something, it will be perfectly ineligible. I declare, you *are* a most provoking creature. Just wait until I present you to some of my friends at Almack's."

"What?" the earl exclaimed. "Do you mean to take her to the marriage mart? Don't raise your and her hopes too high, Lavinia."

"And pray why not?" demanded the affronted widow. "Her countenance is quite pleasing, and she is well born and bred. There is no reason why she shouldn't take."

The earl raised his quizzing glass again and subjected Aurora to a close scrutiny. The way his eyes traveled up and down her body caused a hot flush to appear on Aurora's cheeks. But his next words sounded almost indifferent. "Oh, she is quite passable, I agree, and with proper clothes might even be striking; but penniless girls are not looked on with favor, however beautiful they might be."

A wave of bitterness swept over Aurora. Having experienced that unpalatable truth at firsthand, she had to agree with him. But there must be someone more honorable than Waldo, someone who could see past her poverty to herself.

"Money, money, money, that's *all* everybody thinks

about!" she exploded. "Not that I expect or wish Lady Lanville to marry me off to some odious boor. But why should money always be the only consideration?"

"My sentiments exactly," Lord Albert approved. "Such lovely ladies as Miss Marshingham and Miss Fant ought not to worry about finding a husband just because they are not plump in the pocket."

"I am not worrying about finding a husband, and Miss Fant is worrying about escaping a potential one," Aurora reminded him.

The earl rose impatiently from his chair. "It seems that I have again wasted my time by coming here, so I shall bid you all good day. You may keep Miss Fant here as you wish, Lavinia, but take care you and Miss Marshingham don't plunge yourselves into a worse fix." He stared at his brother, his brows drawn together, then he shook his head, as if ridding himself of some notion. His searching gaze fell on Aurora, who withstood his probing stare with tolerable composure, although her cheeks slowly became suffused with red once again. Suddenly he looked away, picked up his gloves, and stalked out of the room in long, swift strides.

- 9 -

SOME TIME LATER that afternoon Aurora at last found herself
alone. Her patience had been much tried by Lady Lanville's
complaints and Melanie's nervousness. But, after a short
rest, Lavinia had been driven off to see a friend and Melanie
had been induced to take to her bed.

Aurora made a call at the Registry Office, but it proved
fruitless, and she began to despair of ever obtaining a position. She must contrive to persuade Lady Lanville to rec-
ommend her to one of her friends, a favor that, up to now,
the widow had refused to perform for her.

In a somewhat subdued mood Aurora took a hackney to
Leicester Square, where she visited several establishments
catering to a lady's wardrobe. At Madame Flandin's she
purchased a simple gown for Melanie. Aurora and Lavinia
had agreed it would have been imprudent of Melanie to
venture out, since she might be seen and recognized.

Melanie's gown was the last purchase on Aurora's list.
By this time she was quite laden with parcels and bandboxes.
Suddenly she recollected that her sister Priscilla's birthday
was the next week. In a fit of extravagance, Aurora bought
her some coquelicot ribbons and a new reticule—and was

71

dismayed to find herself left without even the small sum to hire a hackney to drive her back to Berkeley Square.

She supposed she could have hired a conveyance and then asked Lady Lanville to pay the jarvey off, but she realized that the widow, not particularly enamoured with the idea of Melanie's stay in Berkeley Square, would not be pleased at having to spend additional money on her two guests. Moreover, she might not be back yet; or if she were, she might not have any pocket money either. So Aurora decided to walk. It wasn't the thing to do, of course, and she hoped she would not be recognized by her ladyship's friends.

But Aurora was not well acquainted with the neighborhood, and in short order she was hopelessly lost. Vexed with herself, she asked directions of a small boy and a fat lady, but the one said to turn to the right, the other to the left, and neither way seemed to be bringing her closer to home.

Several strutting bucks showed themselves quite willing to help her carry her parcels, and even to drive her home, but she would not trust them or their directions. She began to fret. She was not precisely afraid, but her arms ached from carrying the bandboxes and parcels, and her own sense of propriety was offended by having to constantly repel unwelcome advances. The neighborhood was getting shabbier and shabbier. Obviously she was heading in the wrong direction. Yet no matter where she turned, the result seemed the same.

To make matters worse, Aurora heard footsteps behind her. An unsavory individual with a slouch seemed to be following her. It was daylight, but thieves and purse snatchers were always easy to come by, especially in the poorer quarters of the town.

Aurora increased her pace, vowing to take the first hackney she clapped her eyes on and worry about paying off the jarvey later. But she came upon not a single hackney stand. Still, the street she was walking along should lead her eventually to Berkeley Square, she reasoned.

That suspicious-looking man was still on her trail. Aurora concluded that he was waiting for her to enter a less populated lane, where he would have more freedom to deal with her. After all, she did not look like a helpless creature—at least she hoped she didn't—and she might put up a disagreeable fight. Aurora gave an impatient sigh and hurried on.

She hardly paid attention when a curricle-and-four swept past her, but she was startled into frozen immobility when a well-known voice shouted her name.

She whirled around.

Lord Roxton was pulling up and beckoning her to come closer.

Relief at seeing a familiar face and a conveyance that would certainly carry her home barely overcame her vexation that she would be obliged to the earl for her rescue.

Roxton, attired in a many-caped driving coat, jumped down from the curricle and went to his horses heads to steady them. "Whatever possessed you to walk these streets alone?" he demanded. "Why didn't you hire a hack or take Lavinia's carriage—if you had to venture out alone?"

"Lady Lanville had gone in her barouche, and I didn't take a hackney for I have no more money to pay the fare. Not that it is any concern of yours," Aurora added, too exhausted to put up much of a fight.

"Ninnyhammer. You could have paid it once you arrived in Berkeley Square."

"With what? Money borrowed from the servants? I haven't been reduced that far yet. Though it may come to that," she added bitterly.

"Not the servants; Lavinia. Get up." But seeing that Aurora would have the greatest difficult doing so, he added abruptly, "Here, let me take those."

Aurora gratefully relinquished her purchases, which he tossed onto the seat, then assisted her into the curricle. He jumped up after her, grabbed the reins and the whip, and lightly felt the restive horses' mouths. The perfectly matched grays plunged forward.

The earl began to chastise her as soon as they were underway. "Of all the imprudent things to do! It is one thing to wander in the park alone, improper though it is, and quite another to venture into this part of town unattended. Have you lost your wits?"

"I was lost," Aurora admitted unwillingly.

The earl nodded. "I thought as much."

"But how did you come to find me?" She could not help wondering.

"I was searching for you," answered the earl.

"What!" Aurora almost scattered her parcels in her astonishment. "Why? And how did you know where to look?"

"I called in Berkeley Square, desirous of having a word with you, and was informed that you had gone out some time ago and had not returned. Bellman, fearing that something had gone amiss, offered me the intelligence that you would be going to Madame Flandin's, so I inquired for you there."

"I am much obliged to you for your solicitude," Aurora said with heavy sarcasm, "but I didn't tell anybody I would walk home."

"No, you didn't. However, you declined Madame Flandin's suggestion of sending a boy to fetch a carriage for you. And when I inquired at the nearest hackney stand, I was told no one answering your description had bespoken a carriage there. But one jarvey remembered a lady overloaded with parcels walking along the street unattended."

"So you drove around looking for me. Pray, why did you take so much trouble with someone you dislike so thoroughly, my lord?"

"I do not dislike you at all, Miss Marshingham. It is your presence in Berkeley Square that I object to."

"Why, then, you'd better persuade Lady Lanville to find me a respectable position with one of her friends, for she positively refuses to do so."

"Is that what you really want?"

"That is what I *must* want, my lord. A woman in my circumstances is offered very little choice. I own I would prefer some other occupation than that of a governess, a schoolmistress, or a companion; but no one would consider a woman for a political post, even if I were of a political turn of mind. I am not clever enough to go on the stage—"

"God forbid!"

"Why? If I had talent in that direction, I certainly would. Oh, I know it would be considered most shocking, but I don't see why a woman cannot remain respectable while enjoying a career on the stage."

"What do you know of such things?" snapped the earl.

"Naturally, I am only a woman, and therefore expected to know nothing. You, my lord, have all the prejudices of the male."

"On the contrary, I begin to see that there *are* women of character who are not simpering little idiots, who do not have the vapors at the slightest provocation, and who are not artful minxes who hide a cold and calculating mind behind a beautiful face."

"Indeed? Am I to understand that it is *my* humble person who has changed your mind? Now you surprise me greatly. I thought I was the lowest creature on earth in your eyes."

The earl's mouth tightened into a hard line as the carriage swept rapidly round a corner. After a moment's silence he spoke with some difficulty. "I may not approve everything you do, but at least you do not become hysterical or threaten me with vapors. Do you honestly think Lavinia or that little goose Melanie are capable of competing in a man's world?"

"Not all women are like Lady Lanville and Melanie. I am persuaded that you must have met at least one lady who was not a watering pot or a simpering miss."

"I've met scores of them—and they all toadeat me to distraction. Tell me, Miss Marshingham, does money really mean nothing to you? I am considered the best prize on the matrimonial mart, if I could but be persuaded to drop the handkerchief. I am saying this without conceit. Yet you have not tried one whit to place yourself in my good graces."

"What—me set a cap for you? I would rather die!" cried Aurora, outraged.

"Am I so revolting to you?"

"My lord, surely you jest. You have given me plainly to understand that in your eyes I am a scheming, vulgar woman, you have insulted me beyond forgiveness—and that was before I had exchanged a dozen words with you. Surely you cannot now expect me to hold you in anything but the strongest aversion. I only wonder at allowing myself to be drawn into conversation with you. Ignoring you would be much more proper."

The earl bit his lip. "I must have been mistaken about your designs on Albert, whatever your relationship with Style. For surely you are intelligent enough to notice that that silly child is head over ears in love with Albert. It's writ plain in her face. If you had wanted him for yourself, you wouldn't have contrived to have Melanie put up in Berkeley Square. For I am sure her stay there is of your contrivance. I only wonder how she fell in love with him in so short a time. She'd hardly clapped eyes on him."

"But her passion is of long standing, or so she informed me. He has been her hero since childhood."

"A schoolroom romance." He frowned. "When could she have— Oh, yes, of course. We visited the manor occasionally. Well, it won't last."

"As to that, I cannot say. But I must tell you that she also saw the viscount at the races, without him being aware of it, and her sentiments then were the same. If anything, they had intensified."

"Surely you don't expect Albert to marry her?" the earl demanded. "I own he seems quite smitten with her, but he is not so lost to all sense of propriety."

"She is of unexceptionable birth. She is a silly little creature, but then Lord Albert would be much more comfortable married to her than to Lady Clara, for instance— from all I have heard of her."

"Clara? I should say not! Of course he could not marry her. Anything would be better than that alliance." He cast her a frowning glance. "You do not know her?"

"No. How should I? I hardly know anybody in town. I've never been out, you see, nor enjoyed a London season."

"Then how did you become acquainted with Lord Style?"

Aurora's lips clamped shut. Were she to tell the earl that it was through Lavinia, he would either tumble on the truth or think her a fast woman to enter into an affair in such a short time. Neither was to be desired. "We shall leave Baron Style out of it, if you please," she said coldly.

"But we can't leave him out of it, thanks to your meddling," the earl said, growing irritable again. "Style is bound to discover that Lavinia is harboring Melanie."

"And that would only make him cross with Lady Lanville. Wouldn't that meet with your approval?"

"Nothing meets with my approval that is contrived in a clandestine fashion," Roxton said with severity.

"It seems to me, my lord, that you worry overmuch about what is none of your concern," Aurora chided him. "Lady Lanville, I, the baron, and even the viscount are all of age and should be left alone to conduct our affairs as we see fit."

"I cannot leave alone a matter that touches on the honor of my family. And the fate of my nephew and niece is very much my concern," he added.

"Very noble and proper, I'm sure, but your nephew is still in shortcoats and your niece hasn't even reached the sampler-sewing stage. They are just children, small children at that. Lady Lanville's friendship with Baron Style cannot harm them."

"Not yet," said the earl grimly. "But I must not let it progress too far. God forbid that that scoundrel should become the children's stepfather."

"Oh? As to that, I am not perfectly sure but I do know that Lord Style is badly in need of money and could hardly support a wife and two children in the style to which they are accustomed, Aurora answered. "I do not know what would happen to Lady Lanville's allowance in the event of her remarriage, but I'm sure the baron knows you, my lord, would make sure he could not lay his hands on any of it."

"I certainly would."

"Then where's the danger from Lord Style? He needs to marry money."

The earl, knitting his brow, gave her a searching glance. "What does Alphonsus mean to you?" he asked abruptly. "You don't hold him in much esteem, I perceive."

"I am not blind, if that is what you mean. I am *not* a ninny." Aurora's blue eyes sparkled with mischief. "I may not have traveled much beyond Yorkshire, but I am considered a good judge of character. And if you mean to ask me why I associate with the baron, pray do not, for I shan't discuss it."

"Obstinate creature! If you do not expect to marry him . . . Surely you cannot be in— No, no, that is not to be thought of. You are far too intelligent to fall for that rogue. Why, he isn't even handsome. Is your association with Lord Style of long standing?" he persisted.

Aurora's eyes flashed with anger. "You are most impertinent, prying into a lady's personal affairs. You do not know how to converse with propriety, nor how to respect someone else's wishes. And you had better pay attention to your horses if you don't want us to overturn."

"What? You dare instruct me in the art of driving!" the earl exclaimed.

"And," Aurora continued coldly, "if you intend to persist in addressing me on the subject of Lord Style, then pray have the goodness to stop the carriage and let me get down. I would rather walk home than be subjected to any more of your prying questions. Isn't it enough for you, my lord, that I shall not stay in Berkeley Square above a sennight? Isn't it enough that you can be perfectly sure now that I have no designs on your brother?" she added with a twinge of bitterness. "I would have thought that *that* was your main concern, *that* was what brought you back so soon to London."

The earl said nothing for a moment, his lips tightening, a faint flush spreading over the handsome face. Then he spoke up, again with difficulty. "If—if indeed you have not set your cap at Albert, as it seems, then I must beg your pardon."

Aurora gave a scornful laugh. "It is a little too late for *that*, my lord. You pry and scold and beg my pardon all in the same breath. I don't consider such an apology adequate."

The color in his face heightened. "What would you have me do? Go on my knees before you? I'm still not perfectly sure about your character, but I admit I may have been wrong about your designs on Albert. I can do no more than beg your pardon for that. As for the rest, your conduct has been reprehensible. Opera masquerades, clandestine meetings in the park—"

"Enough! Enough said, my lord," cried Aurora. "You can't ever open your mouth without insulting me, even when you try to apologize. Pray stop this carriage at once and let me alight. I do not desire to remain in your company an instant longer."

"Unfortunately we are already there," the earl said, pulling up the horses.

Aurora blinked. She had been so preoccupied with her dispute with the earl that she had not realized they had reached Berkeley Square. The earl leaped from the curricle and offered her his hand, but Aurora declined his offer and prepared to jump down by herself. However, while she was still contemplating how to accomplish that with her arms full of parcels, the earl resolved her dilemma for her by lifting her bodily from the carriage and setting her down. Aurora was not a small woman, but he handled her as if she were made of feathers. In spite of this cavalier treatment of her, the brief contact made her body tingle pleasurably.

Before she had an opportunity to express her outrage at his effrontery, he said, "Spare me any more of your homilies. For once show that good sense that I know you possess and leave those scathing words unspoken. We don't want to present a spectacle for the servants."

About to retort hotly, Aurora perceived that the door of Lady Lanville's house was open and that a worried footman was hurrying out. Behind him appeared Stobbins' impassive face. Aurora relinquished her parcels into the footman's hands.

"Thank God you are safe, miss. Lady Lanville was so worried and that young lady abovestairs has wakened and is near tears and—"

"Look after my horses," the earl commanded curtly.

"My parcels!" cried Aurora.

"Permit me, miss." Stobbins, bowing to the earl, removed the parcels from the footman and, carrying them, ushered her and the earl inside.

- 10 -

IN THE HALL they were met by an exceedingly agitated Lady Lanville.

"Aurora, you ungrateful girl. Where have you been? I've been driven to distraction! When I came home and received the news that you had not yet returned and Roxton was looking for you— And that child is having hysterics! Oh, I nearly *swooned!* Where have you been? Where did you find her, Roxton?"

"Walking the streets alone, with her arms full of parcels, an easy prey to any passing buck or a footpad," the earl answered her darkly.

The widow gave a hysterical shriek. "How could you do something so foolhardly, Aurora? You of all people, usually so sensible! And why did it take you so long? I didn't think you had more than half a dozen errands."

"I bought some presents for Priscilla, my sister. It's her birthday soon. And I stopped at the Registry Office to see whether they had a position available."

"Merciful heaven!" Lavinia clapped her hands together. "You do not give up! You really wish to be a governess. Why don't you wait at least until after Almack's?"

"I suggest it would be more proper to discuss these matters in the parlor, Lavinia," the earl said with icy politeness as he took off his hat and coat.

Lavinia did not pay him the slightest attention. "I am distraught! Whatever will Aunt Martha say? A Marshingham of Treeton Hall reduced to seeking a menial position. It does not bear thinking of!"

Suddenly the earl stiffened. "Treeton Hall? Did you say Treeton Hall? Miss Marshingham, is that true?"

Aurora drew herself up. "Yes, indeed it is. My father was Lord Treeton. But I do not see anything shameful in my seeking employment."

The earl rubbed his forehead. "Treeton Hall . . . Treeton . . . Was your father a widower?"

"Yes."

"And Sir Boniface Cudsworth was the executor of your father's will."

"Yes, he was." Aurora was surprised. "I see that you are more acquainted with my circumstances than I was aware of. If indeed you are so cognizant, then you must also know that it was all Sir Boniface's fault that I and my sisters were left penniless after Papa's death. It was he who mismanaged what was left of the estate so dreadfully that we were forced to sell Treeton Hall and all the lands. If it hadn't been for Aunt Martha and Uncle Horace, we would have been turned out onto the streets."

The earl looked mortified. Both Aurora and Lavinia stared at him in puzzlement as a circle of curious servants surrounded them.

Abruptly the earl recollected his surroundings. His mouth hardened. "Off with you. Begone to your duties," he rounded on the servants. "Let us go into the parlor. I must talk to you, Miss Marshingham."

"What about? I don't see why you seem so affected by the information you have just received."

The earl did not answer until they were all in the yellow salon with the doors closed against prying ears.

Aurora began to strip off her gloves while Lavinia tottered to the sofa, moaning and sniffing at her vinaigrette.

The earl took an impatient turn about the room. "I had no idea—It happened just before Will died, and that drew everything else from my mind. Afterward"—he rubbed his brow—"afterward I must have forgotten, or else I thought things didn't come out too badly. I never asked Sir Boniface about it, as concerned as I was with other matters."

"What is it, my lord? You have me in quite a puzzle," Aurora said sitting down in a yellow-and-gold upholstered armchair. "I cannot conceive why my tale is so disturbing to you."

The earl's countenance was pale and harsh.

"Boniface Cudsworth is some sort of an uncle of mine," he said in a self-accusing tone.

"Oh," cried Lavinia. "Oh, yes. Now I recall. Of course, that odd creature who was present at our—I mean my and Will's—wedding. I haven't clapped eyes on him since. But pray, why should that upset you so? You are not held accountable for your uncle's actions. Moreover, I collect, you don't see each other very often."

"No. We meet at White's occasionally, or at St. James's. But the point is—" He stared at Aurora oddly. "You really didn't *know*? You didn't know Sir Boniface was my uncle before you decided to visit Lavinia?"

"What rubbish! I didn't even *decide* to visit Lavinia. It was something she and Aunt Martha thought up."

"You did not come to London with thoughts of revenge?"

"Revenge! Revenge on whom, my lord? You, or Lady Lanville? Indeed, Lord Roxton, I did not expect hearing *you* talk such fustian."

Lavinia regarded the earl with lively astonishment. "Don't pay him any heed, Aurora. He must have a touch of the sun. Whyever should you want to take revenge on us?"

"You do not know," repeated the earl in the same self-accusing tone. "You do not know that I was perfectly aware that Sir Boniface was not fit to arrange anyone's financial matters, let alone an encumbered estate."

"And what if you did know? You weren't the executor of Papa's will or the manager of his estates. You had no say in the matter."

"Oh, but I had." The earl seemed genuinely anguished. "You see, Sir Boniface turned to *me* in his predicament. He felt unable to cope and heartily wished Lord Treeton had not left his estate in his care. Sir Boniface told me he was

quite at a loss as to how to settle the estate. He asked for
my help and advice. I, knowing only too well what a sad
botch he could make of things, half promised him I would
help. But then Will had the accident and died; I had his
affairs to settle, and Sir Boniface and his predicament
slipped from my mind. He didn't urge me to advise him any
more. I suppose he realized I was too much"—his lips
pressed in pain for a moment—"too much affected by Will's
death to be bothered with other matters. Come to think of
it, I didn't see him above once or twice after Will's funeral,
and then we merely exchanged a passing nod. So he tried
to settle Lord Treeton's affairs himself, without my help,
and made a sad muddle of it."

"A sad muddle is putting it very mildly," cried Aurora,
barely able to grasp the enormity of the earl's disclosure.
Finally she found her voice. "I might have known all our
troubles could be laid at your door, my lord."

"No, no, Aurora," Lavinia expostulated feebly, though
she was as shocked as Aurora over this revelation. "You
cannot blame Roxton for your papa's poor choice of an
executor. As for not helping Sir Boniface—it is not to be
wondered at, we were at such sixes and sevens at that time.
You must own it would have been most difficult for him
to pay attention to anything but his brother's family."

Aurora jumped up from her seat. "I own nothing of the
kind." She swept past Roxton, her head held high but her
chin trembling. "Do not try to convince me of your good
intentions, my lord. I do not want to hear another word. I
am heartily sick of your explanations."

She marched out of the room, but Roxton's harsh voice
stopped her cold at the foot of the staircase.

"One moment, Miss Marshingham. I want a word with
you."

She whirled. "But I do not wish to speak with you."

He was across the hall in a trice, barring her way. His
powerful hand grasped her wrist.

"Pray let me go, Lord Roxton."

"Not until you hear me out." He led her to a settee at
the side of the staircase. The hall was deserted, not a servant
in sight. Reluctantly, Aurora sat down beside him.

"Miss Marshingham," he began slowly, his face impassive but his voice betraying some strong inner feeling. "Miss Marshingham, you do not know how deeply I regret the unfortunate turn of events that has placed you in these straitened circumstances. I beg you to believe that I would have done all in my power to insure that my Uncle Boniface did not mismanage Lord Treeton's estate, were it not for the untimely . . . demise of my brother. We were very close, Will and I, and in my grief I simply could not spare a thought for anything or anyone."

"Apologies won't help now," Aurora said stiffly. "That is water under the bridge."

"Pray hear me to the end, ma'am, and you shall understand. As . . . as a result of my neglect, you find yourself obliged to seek employment—a thought not to be borne for the daughter of Lord Treeton."

"If *I* can bear it, my lord, so can you. And if, as I collect, you will try persuading me to agree to Lady Lanville's scheme, you are wasting my time and yours. I am only surprised that you think it would serve, were I willing to go along with it. Who from all these fine gentlemen would offer for a penniless unknown? If you excuse me, my lord—" She began to rise.

A shade of annoyance crossed the earl's countenance. "One moment, please, Miss Marshingham!" he said in a sharp tone. "Pray allow me to finish."

Aurora subsided. "Very well."

"Much as I dislike my sister-in-law, I must agree with her that a respectable marriage to a gentleman of sufficient means to provide for both you and your sisters is the only acceptable solution to your problem."

"But—"

The earl put up a hand. "I am well aware that it would be a marriage of convenience, but it would provide you and your sisters with all the necessaries that your birth entitles you to, and would enable you to take your rightful place in society."

"Very pretty, my lord. And even—even suppose that I were willing to agree to such an outrageous proposal, where would I find a gentleman willing to take on three penniless girls for the sake of a marriage with one of them? Pray, tell me what, short of a severe infatuation, would compel a gentleman to take such a foolhardy step."

"To a gentleman of means, the support of three ladies, be they ever so expensive, would not be much of a drain on his pocket."

"Oh, this is all—"

"Permit me to continue, ma'am." The earl's lips pressed tight for a second.

"Then come right to the point, my lord. You seem to be getting to it in a very roundabout way."

The earl drew in a deep breath. "As you wish. I have just told you that, feeling greatly responsible for being the unwitting cause of your misfortune, I am deeply concerned about your fate and am determined to make the only restitution that would be adequate under the circumstances." He paused.

"And that is?" Aurora prompted.

"And that is, Miss Marshingham, to offer you or one of your sisters the protection of my name and fortune."

Aurora gasped. The color receded from her cheeks. "You—you mean . . . ? Is this a proposal of marriage, my lord?" she asked in a strangled voice.

"It is," said the earl. His tone was level now, but his face was pale.

Aurora felt the room whirl about her. To be married to *him*. For a moment the thought took her breath away. Then revulsion set in. His opinion of her had not changed. He was offering her marriage out of guilt and pity, not love. In his own way he was just as bad as Waldo. And to think for a moment she had—

"Well, of all the infamous things!" The words burst from her suddenly dry lips.

"As I am only too well aware in what aversion you hold my person," the earl continued, "I suggest that perhaps one of your sisters would do me the honor of becoming my wife."

"Adelina is still in the schoolroom, and nothing, but *nothing* would induce Priscilla to marry you, even were she not madly in love with some completely ineligible soldier.

Moreover, she has too much sensibility to countenance your rough and odious ways."

"I would promise not to interfere."

"It would never answer. You'd as lief be married to Melanie or Lady Lanville."

Annoyance spread over the earl's face.

"Vapors. An exceedingly nervous disposition," explained Aurora. "She would vex you to death, and you would scare her out of her wits. My lord, such a proposal is an affront to our name. It is the greatest insult—"

"I do not think that the offer of my name and fortune is an insult," snapped the earl. "Please reconsider Miss Marshingham. If you can't stomach me as a husband, better let your sister marry me. I would let her go her own way, and I would go mine, and all three of you would secure a future."

Aurora rose stiffly. "Indeed, my lord, I cannot agree to such a proposal. I could write about it to Priscilla, but I know full well what her answer would be. As for myself, nothing could prevail upon me to accept your—your charity! I would rather scrub floors than call myself Lady Roxton."

One of the earl's brows rose. "That is doing it too brown, ma'am. That is more in Lavinia's style, not yours. You have far too much sense for such wild talk."

Aurora was momentarily taken aback. "Very well, but ... but it is no exaggeration, my lord, that I find you the most insulting and overbearing man alive. Indeed, I am surprised you can even contemplate marriage with someone like myself. I well remember the handsome epithets you bestowed on me."

Chagrin flittered over the earl's visage. "That was before I knew you were Lord Treeton's daughter; and you must own that your conduct—"

"My conduct, my conduct! If you, my lord, were not so rash in jumping to conclusions— But that's all to no purpose. You have said your piece, now pray let me go."

The earl gave her a stiff bow. "Very well. If that is what you wish."

"That is what I wish. There is nothing more to be said between us."

The earl bowed again. "Once again I beg you to reconsider my offer. I shall speak to you about it in the near future."

- *11* -

AURORA HAD SUFFERED at the earl's hands, but worse was yet to come. In the afternoon of the following day, the baron paid a call in Berkeley Square. Lord Roxton's spy, whoever he was, would be bound to bear the tale to the earl. But for once Lavinia let the baron persuade her.

Aurora had learned that Lavinia had told Style everything—and that he was delighted with the turn of events concerning Melanie. Clearly Albert was in love with the chit. Style considered it a personal victory. For years he'd been trying to win back his family estates. Now, believing Roxton would never marry and that Albert, soon Melanie's husband, would fall heir to all, he was overjoyed.

The baron was ensconced in the yellow salon, rubbing his hands and remarking to Melanie on what a fine-looking pair she and Albert would make. Melanie blushed and stammered and protested feebly, but Style, lounging in an armchair, one elegantly clad leg crossed over the other, was taking snuff and ogling Aurora and Melanie through his quizzing glass, while he regaled Lady Lanville with his dreams for the future.

Aurora found his boasting distasteful, and Melanie found it embarrassing, but Lavinia seemed to have been forcibly struck by the thought that, once the baron had become her brother-in-law, even Roxton could not forbid him to visit her. Not to be obliged to meet Alphonsus clandestinely would be a great relief to her ladyship, and Aurora could sympathize with her feelings. But to disregard Lord Roxton's say in the matter of his brother's marriage, and the disastrous consequences such marriage plans would surely provoke seemed to her both imprudent and dangerous.

Shortly after she had joined Lavinia and the others in the yellow salon, Stobbins entered to announce Lord Roxton, who burst in unceremoniously, stopping short on the threshold upon perceiving the occupants of the room. Naturally his gaze was drawn first to Lord Style. A deep scowl marred his handsome features, his lips pressed into a harsh line of disapproval. "How dare you show your blackguard's face in this house, Style!" he thundered, striding quickly toward the baron.

Baron Style blanched but stood his ground. "This is not your house, Roxton."

"It is my brother's house, my brother's whose death you have caused—"

"No, no!" cried Lavinia. "Do not say so. It is unjust. Do not blame Alphonsus for being here. I invited him. It is *my* house, and if I choose to invite Alphonsus, that is entirely my own affair."

"You will find it is very much my concern when I pack you off to Roxton Hall for the remainder of the London season."

"No. You wouldn't! You couldn't!"

"Oh, wouldn't I?"

"You, my dear Roxton," drawled the baron, "had better become reconciled to my presence in this house, for when Melanie marries your brother—"

"That shall never happen!" the earl interjected grimly.

"I don't think it is in your power to prevent it."

"You underestimate me, Style. Take your wheyfaced chit of a sister back to where she came from and let me never see her face or yours here again."

"My lord, consider Miss Fant's feelings." Aurora was forced to intercede.

"I shall thank you not to interfere again." The earl

rounded on her. "If you had not meddled in what was none of your business, if you had not persuaded Lavinia to keep the chit here, all this would not have happened."

"Oh, pray . . . do not . . . I beg you," stammered Melanie. "I wouldn't for the world . . . I shall not stay here. I—"

"Of course you shall not stay here," replied the earl. "Pack your things if you have any, and take yourself off. I was inclined to regard you as just a silly creature, but I am now of the opinion that you are a shameless baggage in league with your brother, who contrived to win my brother's sympathy. You—"

"No, no, pray say no more," Melanie uttered, white-faced, as large tears rolled down her cheeks. "You cannot— I am not so—That is not true. Oh—" She jumped from the sofa and, covering her face with her hands, rushed from the room.

"Now see what you have done," Aurora cried reproachfully. "I had better go after her."

Baron Style's countenance darkened with rage. "How dare you insult my sister! She is a Lady of Quality, gently nurtured and unused to your boorish ways."

"Hah!" exclaimed Roxton.

"Roxton, Alphonsus, no," cried Lavinia. "I beg you. Oh, how could you—" As the baron got up and took a step toward the earl, she added, "No, no! Alphonsus, pray think what you are about to do."

"What? Do you intend to call me out?" sneered the earl.

"Roxton, Alphonsus! Oh, I am distracted. Alphonsus, I beg you, do not call him out! He is by far the better shot."

"Don't be afraid," the earl replied. "He won't. He is much too cowardly for that."

An ugly look crept into the baron's usually benevolent countenance. "You shall find you are mistaken, my lord," he warned.

"No, no, Alphonsus, I implore you," screamed Lavinia, throwing herself between the two men. She grabbed Lord Style by the arm. "Don't, you cannot. I pray, don't! Oh, I shall have a spasm!" She looked around the room for help. "Aurora, where are you going? Do something!"

"I think Miss Fant requires me more than you do," Aurora answered, going to the door. "I shall send Bellman to you."

"No, no. I don't want her. No one must know."

"You are mistaken if you think the servants are not listening at the keyhole," the earl said sarcastically.

"Then I wonder you provoked this scene, being aware of this, my lord," Aurora said tartly. "Your consequence is such that anything can be forgiven you, as I recollect you have said; but that you want the whole world to know of this—this—"

"Now, don't *you* start," the earl cried in utter exasperation. "Nobody will know anything, nobody will say anything. The servants in Berkeley Square are loyal to the memory of my late brother and their master."

Here the baron interrupted. "I will not have you insult my sister, and I will not let you bully Lavinia any longer!"

"Don't *you* start enacting a Cheltenham tragedy, Style. I will not duel with you, but I can and will plant you a facer if you persist in making yourself a damned nuisance."

"You have no right to insult my sister," the baron persisted.

"If she is just your dupe and not your willing accomplice, I shall beg her pardon. As for Lavinia, she is my sister-in-law, and it is my duty to insure she remains a fit mother to my brother's children, however unpalatable she may find my 'interference.' I owe it to our family's name to—"

"Oh, stop it!" Lavinia interrupted. "You talk as if I were an inferior person, wholly unsuited to bring up my own children, and—and as if my inviting Alphonsus here was some kind of a crime. Have you forgotten, Roxton, that I was affianced to him once?"

"No, I have not forgotten," the earl said through his teeth. "And I wish to God you had married him instead of my brother."

"That can still be remedied," said the baron.

The earl took a threatening step forward. Lavinia turned red, then paled considerably and fell back against the cushions. "Oh, Alphonsus," she moaned, closing her eyes.

The baron was beside her in a trice. "Hartshorn, vinegar! Where are her smelling salts? Miss Marshingham." He turned to Aurora, who was still standing by the door, trying to follow these interchanges. "Pray be so kind as to ring for her ladyship's maid." He began fanning Lavinia.

The earl cast them a disgusted look and turned abruptly on his heel. "Pray have the goodness, ma'am," he said to Aurora, "to see to it that the house is restored to some semblance of sanity before I return. I shall leave now, but I shall be back within half an hour, and I trust I shall not find the baron here." He strode out of the room, muttering under his breath something about Bedlam and hysterical females. The door slammed shut behind him.

A moment later an indignant Bellman rushed into the salon to help succor her mistress. Aurora turned to the baron. "Lord Style, I beg you to leave. It is the only prudent course for you to follow. I shall look after your sister until you decide what is to be done about her. Lady Lanville will contrive, I'm sure, to let you know when it would be safe for you to call again in Berkeley Square."

"I shall not flee from Roxton. I do not fear him," said Alphonsus Fant manfully.

"To be sure, to be sure," Aurora soothed. "But it would not do at all to create a brawl. You must consider her ladyship's feelings, my lord. Now I shall go to your sister. I assure you I will do all I can to calm her, and I will not let his lordship or anybody else bully her; but you had best leave, Lord Style."

She hurried out of the room and up the staircase to the bedchamber alloted to Melanie Fant.

It took Aurora some time to quiet that agitated damsel, but at last she persuaded her to swallow a few drops of laudanum. When at last the young girl fell into an exhausted slumber, Aurora tiptoed out of the room, wondering what had happened belowstairs. The house was strangely quiet; no servants were about as she knocked softly on Lady Lanville's chamber door.

A feeble voice bade her enter.

Lady Lanville was reclining on her bed, a wet cloth on her brow, the vinaigrette in her hand.

"I thought it was Bellman with the tea," she moaned upon seeing Aurora. "Aurora, I shall *never* forgive you for deserting me when I needed you so badly. That silly girl didn't need your help as much as I did. The things Roxton said to me—"

"You mean he came back?"

"Of course he came back," said the affronted widow, fanning herself. "And he had the temerity and the—the indelicacy to invade my bedchamber, only to command me—not beg or ask, but to command me—to send Melanie packing first thing tomorrow morning. Not that I mind doing that, for the girl is nothing but trouble to us, but the tone he used—as if it were my fault the child was here. And then he informed me that he will be obliged to send me up to Roxton Hall. Roxton Hall! At the *height* of the season! I couldn't *bear* it. I just *couldn't*.

"Only one thing could induce that odious man not to carry out his threat," she continued, "and that would be for Albert to reassure him that Melanie means nothing more to him than a passing fancy; that he has just taken pity on the girl and Alphonsus has jumped to the wrong conclusion. Oh, we must persuade Albert not to think about the chit any more. Not that I think his feelings could have become seriously engaged in such a short time. Although I myself, the minute I clapped eyes on Alphonsus for the first time . . ." A slight color suffused her cheeks. "But that's neither here nor there. We must send a note to Albert, ask him to come round and—"

"I do not think that would be wise when Melanie is still here," cautioned Aurora. She sighed. "I own I thought it would be good for the two to marry, but I see that it just won't do, not with Roxton so violently opposed to the match."

The widow shuddered. "Of course it would not do. Not that I would mind. I would even be inclined to favor the match. But to be sent up to Roxton Hall . . . No, no, that is not to be thought of." She sank back on her pillows. "I *declare*, I haven't had a moment's peace since you entered this house, Aurora."

Aurora stiffened. "I shall not be here much longer. If I cannot find a suitable post soon, I shall remove to Yorkshire."

Lady Lanville uttered a shriek. "Never say you would do that! No, no. There is the ball for the grand duchess. Oh, how can you be so provoking! I shall have another spasm this instant."

"Then I had better leave you to enjoy it in private,"

Aurora said, turning to the door. "I shall send Bellman to you." Disregarding her cousin's protests, she marched out of the room, two red spots burning on her cheeks, her bosom heaving with humiliation.

She would not remain in Berkeley Square any longer. If no post offered itself within a few days, she would take the next mailcoach home. Thus resolved, and with unwelcome tears pricking her eyelids, Aurora slowly returned to her room.

- *12* -

AFTER LORD ROXTON'S ultimatum, Aurora had to endure enough vapors and hysterics from Melanie and Lavinia to last her a lifetime. Melanie Fant was sent back to her boarding school, but not without violent protests from Lord Albert, who insisted that she should be allowed to stay in Berkeley Square. It took all Aurora's skills of persuasion to convince the viscount that sending Melanie back was the only sensible course to follow. They could always invite her again, once Lord Roxton's anger had abated, or when he'd left town. As for urging the viscount to cease being concerned in Melanie's welfare, Aurora judged it was not the time to insist upon that. His ardor must be given time to cool, she reasoned.

Aurora's own attempts at finding a post ended in failure, and with a heavy heart she began to pack her belongings, determined to leave for Yorkshire on the next Mail.

While Aurora was thus engaged one afternoon shortly after Melanie's departure, Lavinia entered her bedchamber. She was dressed for going out. A fetching hat was perched at a rakish angle on her elaborately arranged blond curls, and she carried a parasol and a reticule in her hand.

"Aurora, I wish you to accompany me to—" She per-

97

ceived Aurora packing and gave a horrified shout. "What are you doing? You are not thinking of leaving us!" she cried.

"Since I have been nothing but trouble to your ladyship, I'd better remove myself from the premises."

"Provoking creature!" The widow stamped her foot. "You *cannot* do that. Not before the grand duchess's ball. And certainly not today. Have you seen Roxton?"

"Thankfully, no."

"Well, I have. He was at his most disagreeable, as you may well conceive, but I contrived to almost convince him that Albert is not seriously interested in Melanie. Now all I have to do is convince Albert of the same. I have tried before, but I was still quite ill and only angered him. I've sent a note round to Brook Street desiring him to come to Berkeley Square, but he has taken one of his rare pets and refuses to come. I very much fear that he might try to see Melanie."

Lavinia took a turn about the room, her voice becoming more high pitched. "You must make him see reason, Aurora, since *you* were responsible for bringing them together. And we must go to his rooms now. Roxton means to go up to Roxton Hall in a few days and if we can't convince him there is no danger of Albert's marrying Melanie, that odious man will insist on my removing to Roxton Hall too."

"You want me to go to the viscount's lodgings, to Brook Street?" Aurora exclaimed.

"Where else? Where else can I—we—talk to him undisturbed and in private?"

"Yes, but—for a lady to go calling on a gentleman..."

The widow stamped her foot again. "Don't start talking to me of proprieties, Aurora. Albert is my brother-in-law. Besides, who's to know of it? No one of my servants, at all events. That's another reason I want you to go with me. I can't go alone, and I don't want to take any of them. We can go in my phaeton; the barouche is being fitted with new squabs. You will have to drive, though, for I'm not up to it yet. Besides, I haven't driven it since Will's death."

"I am surprised to hear of your driving a phaeton at all."

"Oh, it's not a perch phaeton. It's an elegant carriage and perfectly proper for dashing ladies of the *ton* to drive.

Will bought it for me, for Elyza Wembly had one and I—But that's to no purpose. Will you go?"

"But you are ready to go now, while I'm not. Why didn't you—"

"Don't say you won't go after putting us all in that fix," Lavinia persisted.

Aurora's lips compressed into a thin line and she bit back a sharp retort. What was the use? Besides, she, Aurora, could be held accountable in some measure for the disastrous events. She suppressed a sigh. "Oh, very well. But I hope we can convince him speedily. I would like to catch the night Mail."

"You cannot mean to do so."

"There is no point in my going to Roxton Hall with you."

"But I don't *wish* to go to Roxton Hall," wailed the widow. "And once we have persuaded Albert to reassure Roxton, I shan't have to. And neither will you. I suppose nothing suitable was offered you today?"

"No."

"Well, if you promise to stay until the grand duchess's ball, I shall see if I can find you a position."

Aurora's eyes lit up. "Oh, would you?" Then suspicious, she asked, "What made you change your mind?"

"I just remembered that Lord Pembury has been widowed this last month. He has a little girl and might be looking for a governess. He is not a bad-looking man, and if you play your cards right . . ."

Aurora had to laugh. "Oh, Lavinia, matchmaking again."

"And why not? I have promised Aunt Martha."

"I wonder that you feel obliged to go to so much trouble for Aunt Martha," Aurora mused aloud.

The widow colored. "Aunt Martha did me a particular favor once." She made a helpless gesture with her hand and abruptly sat down on the bed. "If you must know, she was the only one of my family and friends who did not object to Alphonsus. In fact, we used to meet in her parlor, if we couldn't contrive to meet elsewhere."

"I can't believe it!" exclaimed Aurora, delighted with this news. Aunt Martha, aiding and abetting young lovers. It was hard to think of the wizened, careworn woman in that role. Yet she had a good heart.

"Then you will go with me? That dress you have on will do quite well," Lavinia added, casting an approving glance at Aurora's gray crepe walking dress. "Just don a bonnet and you might want to take a cloak, although it is a particularly warm day."

"Lavinia," Aurora asked suddenly, "why didn't you marry Lord Style?"

Lavinia gave a mournful sigh. "Several reasons, I suppose. The family was all against it, and Alphonsus had not a feather to fly with. And then I met Will. And I—I suppose I fell out of love with Alphonsus and in love with him. Will was such a grand gentleman and so rich and attentive. And quite handsome. Not that Alphonsus isn't handsome too." Aurora raised a skeptical eyebrow. "But Will was different, and the family, especially Mama, was transported with delight. He was so amiable and so eligible. He was a friend of Alphonsus's too, and for a while I felt dreadfully guilty throwing Alphonsus over for Will. But Alphonsus understood. He has a great many faults, but he always understands my feelings perfectly.

"Now shall we go?" she said. "Put on your bonnet. Come, for he may go off somewhere. He likes to have his afternoon tea at home, but you never know where a gentleman's fancy might take him. Let us go immediately."

Aurora threw the rest of the things she had spread out on her bed into the portmanteau, straightened her hair, tied on a bonnet, and, grabbing her cloak, followed Lavinia out to the carriage.

The day was warm, the sky blue. In spite of her troubles, Aurora's spirits brightened when contemplating the beauty of nature. Somehow she would contrive to get herself out of her difficulties and provide a future for herself and her sisters.

The women drew up before the Viscount Deberough's house; Aurora jumped down and helped Lavinia to alight. The front door was opened to them by a footman, who regretfully informed them that the viscount was from home.

"Then we shall wait for him," Lavinia declared. "He must return shortly, for I remember he promised to attend Mrs. Wedgeborough's party, and he would have to change." She pushed past the startled servant, and Aurora followed, desiring the man to have someone look after the horses.

The footman ushered them into the parlor and, after politely asking them if they required any refreshments, withdrew.

Aurora seated herself on a sofa, admiring the elegant pink-and-gold decor of the room and idly thinking that Melanie would have been delighted to be the mistress of such a fine establishment. But Lavinia was too restless to sit down. After stripping off her gloves, she paced the room with quick, nervous strides. "No, indeed! It is too provoking of Albert." she complained. "It's as if he knew I—we— were to call on him and left the house just to disoblige me."

"I am persuaded it is nothing of the kind," soothed Aurora. "And I doubt we should wait for him. He might be gone for hours."

"Never say that! I *must* talk to him. And he is usually so amiable and obliging. Indeed, it is *too* bad for him."

Stopping by the mantelpiece, she glanced idly at the mail deposited there. "Good heavens," she exclaimed abruptly, "that's the Duke of Hartford's calling card! I was not aware Albert was acquainted with the duke. And that,"—she picked up a pink missive sealed with a wafer and sniffed it—"from Clara Carswell, no doubt. That's her scent." She dropped the letter, strode to a winged armchair by the fireplace, and plunked herself down. She jumped up again almost immediately. Her restless fingers returned to the mantelpiece.

"Just look at that scrawl," she said, picking up another letter. "Looks like somebody just out of the schoolroom. Oh, it wasn't properly sealed. It's open! Now, I wonder who it could be from." She began to fold the paper together when suddenly she stiffened. "Oh, no! It's Melanie Fant!" she exclaimed. "I *must* read it, Aurora. Oh, dear, I know I oughtn't, but I—"

"No, I don't think you should read a gentleman's mail," Aurora responded curtly.

"Well, I wasn't. It was imperfectly sealed and came open in my hands. Oh, dear, she addresses him as her only friend. Fancy that."

"Lavinia, put that letter down!" Aurora said sharply.

"Yes, yes. But I wonder what she can be writing to him

about. It might be providential that it came open. Oh, great heavens!" Lavinia's eyes started from their sockets. Then completely disregarding Aurora's protests, she continued to peruse the missive to the end.

"What a disaster!" she moaned, clutching the letter. "Oh, it is the *worst* thing that could have happened. Indeed it *is* providential that we found it, for Albert must never read it, *never!*"

"What?" cried Aurora, scandalized. "Really, Lavinia, you are going too far."

"Yes, but only think. That creature wants Albert to help her." Lavinia was growing hysterical.

"What if she does?"

"You don't understand. Here, you had better read it." She profferred the letter to Aurora.

"No, thank you," Aurora said coldly. *"I* do not read other people's mail."

"Well, don't think that *that* is a habit with me. But it is just a piece of good luck that I did. Just think, that chit wants Albert to run after her and rescue her—today and immediately!"

"Rescue her from what?" Aurora was curious in spite of herself. "And why didn't she ask the baron for help? He is the proper person—"

"Well, he won't. I don't say he approves of Gretna Green marriages but he is so—"

"What!" Aurora almost jumped up in her seat.

"But he is so desperate for Melanie to make a profitable match—"

"Who is contemplating a Gretna Green marriage with Melanie?" Aurora interrupted. "Lord Burgley?"

"No, no, no. It's old Silverdale. I wonder where he has seen the chit. Probably at Alphonsus's place. He is just wild enough to do something shatterbrained like that. And he is fifty if he is a day."

"But what did he do, precisely?"

"Do? Do? Just *kidnapped* Melanie and constrained her against her will to flee to the border with him. The girl wants Albert to overtake them and rescue her. And that must *never* happen," she wailed. "That would be just the sort of romantic notion that would appeal to Albert. And

Roxton would never forgive me if he got wind of it. I must destroy the letter."

"Lavinia!"

"Well, what will you have me do? I *cannot* allow Albert to chase after that Fant girl. You realize how disastrous it would be if Albert were to go after them. Oh, it is not to be thought of!"

"I think it is not to be thought of that a young girl just out of the schoolroom should be forced to go through a Gretna Green ceremony with a man old enough to be her father."

"But what can *I* do about it?" asked Lavinia.

"You, nothing. Leave it to Lord Albert."

"I can't."

"Then ask Baron Style."

"No, it won't serve. He'll just upbraid me. He is not pleased with the way things have turned out for him and—"

"Well, somebody should go and rescue that poor girl. Does she say when they set out?" Aurora asked.

"Yes. If Albert were to start after them immediately, he might catch up with them before nightfall. Oh, dear, do you think somebody should go and rescue that troublesome girl?"

"Certainly. Every feeling is offended at such an escapade."

"Well, on no account must it be Albert," Lavinia said. "Who else is there beside ourselves?"

"Lord Roxton?" Aurora suggested. "No. He would not bestir himself on behalf of the baron's sister."

"That leaves only us," the widow moaned.

"Yes. It seems there are only two courses left for you. Leave the letter for Lord Albert to find, or go after the girl yourself—if you cannot think of anyone else whom you could ask to go in his stead."

"Go myself?" shrieked Lady Lanville.

Aurora sprang up from the sofa impatiently. "Oh, put that letter on the mantelpiece and let us leave."

"No! Albert must not see it." Lavinia slipped it into her reticule.

"Well! If you can allow that girl to be dragged to the

anvil with a clear conscience—"

"No, no. Of course I don't wish that to happen. He would catch up with them before nightfall, if he were to start out now," she mused. "Oh, dear, how *very* vexing. I suppose I shall have to go after them. It is not at all proper for a lady to—Oh, dear, I do not wish at all to be embroiled in such an affair."

"Then leave it to Lord Albert," Aurora retorted.

"No. There is no one else I can turn to in this fix."

"How about the servants?" Aurora inquired.

"What? And have one of them rushing to Roxton to apprise him of it the instant? I might as well tell it to the town crier," Lavinia added bitterly. "I wish I knew the identity of the spy in my household. But there is only one thing to be done. We shall go at once."

"What? You want *me* to go too? I suppose you can hardly go unaccompanied but—" Aurora still intended to take the Mail that night.

"Aren't you willing to help me, Aurora? Or are you just good at advising *others* to do something, which *you* would rather not do?"

"But we can't go now, just like that. We're not dressed for it."

"Oh, fiddle! It's a warm day, and the horses are fresh. Of course *you* will have to drive, but I'm sure you will not mind." Lavinia was preparing to leave.

Aurora heaved a sigh. "No, no. I won't mind. But in an open carriage . . . Oh, very well. Let us go after the pair, by all means. But won't Martha and Tom be upset if you don't kiss them good night?"

"No, they'll just think their mama is indisposed again. Depend upon it, Nurse won't let them know I haven't returned. Besides, if we hurry, we might contrive to be back in Berkeley Square before supper."

"I doubt it," Aurora said. She shook her head. "I do hope we are doing the right thing not to let Lord Albert know about it."

"Of course we are. We are doing it for his own good as well as ours." And she swept out of the room.

- *13* -

THE SUN WAS setting when Lavinia and Aurora, dusty, disheveled, and tired, approached yet another postinghouse on the Great North Road in their search for the fugitives.

"I don't care if we find them here or not," moaned Lady Lanville upon catching sight of the inn. "I cannot travel any farther. I must have some rest and refreshment. I hope they have something more decent to drink than ale or that unpalatable brew they called tea at the Blue Hart."

"It was the Blue Boar," answered Aurora.

"Oh, what's the odds!" snapped the widow, fanning herself, then abruptly pulling Aurora's cloak closer about her. "And the air has turned chilly. It will soon be dark," she moaned.

"If you had not insisted on resting at practically every postinghouse we came upon, we would have progressed much faster." Aurora could scarcely conceal her irritation.

"But how was I to know I would become so excessively fatigued? Indeed it is too bad of you to blame me for our slow progress. If we had spirited horses, we would catch up with them at Barnet."

"I have grave doubts of catching up with them at all." Aurora sighed. "They must be miles ahead of us. At the rate *we* are traveling, we should consider ourselves lucky to reach Welwyn before nightfall."

"Never say so!" cried Lavinia. "That is too dreadful to contemplate!"

Aurora brought the horses to a halt. An ostler came running out to offer his services.

"I advise you not to stop here but push on—or put up here for the night," Aurora admonished her cousin. "We can't be junketing about at night on the Great North Road, dressed in nothing but our walking dresses and with no gentleman to protect us."

The widow gave a dramatic gasp and cast a furtive glance about her. "Do you think we might be set upon?"

"I don't know," said Aurora tartly. She was cold, hungry, and cross. "No, we shall not alight, my good man," she told the ostler. "Pray tell us only whether a post-chaise-and-four carrying an older gentleman and a very young damsel has passed this way. The damsel is about seventeen, with light hair and very large green eyes."

The ostler nodded. "Aye, ma'am. They passed this way right enough. In a proper hurry they was. Leastways the gentleman was."

"Thank you. That is all we wanted to know. We shall be on our way." Aurora flipped her whip, and the horses moved forward."

The sun had set, the night had fallen, and still the two ladies had not caught up with the fugitives.

"I am cold," Lavinia moaned. "Very likely I shall take a chill and die of inflammation of the lungs! What shall we do? We can't travel any longer. It's pitch dark, and the moon isn't even out."

"If you had not insisted on having the cook prepare a special meal for you at the last stop, we—"

"No, no." Lavinia clutched her heart. "Have you no sensibility? To upbraid me, when you see how much I suffer. And it is all *your* fault too for—"

"Yes, yes, I know." Aurora gave an angry twang with the whip, her temper getting the better of her. "We must reach the next town. At least we are still on their trail. You should be thankful for that."

"I am beginning to think that this is all a hum. A hoax. That there has been no abduction."

Aurora turned to stare at Lavinia, although it was too dark to distinguish her features. "Whatever do you mean?" she demanded sharply. "We have been told at each posting-house that they have passed through."

"I know, I know. But the more I think of it, the more I'm convinced that this is some sort of a trick."

"Why? Why should you think that now?"

"Because I have just recalled something that I would have recalled before—if I hadn't been so agitated by that letter. The latest *on-dit* is that old Silverdale has been casting out lures to the Leighton girl. It stands to reason he wouldn't elope with Melanie if that is the case."

"You know nothing of the sort. At any rate, we cannot turn back now. It's much nearer to the next postinghouse than to the last one."

"We shall have to spend the night there, and I don't even have a nightgown," Lavinia complained.

"The innkeeper's wife will provide you with one, I'm sure."

"Some rough, dirty linen. Ugh! And the sheets will not be properly aired and—"

"No need to trouble ourselves on that score until we see them," said Aurora impatiently. At that moment, and in spite of her excessive dislike of him, she felt herself again in sympathy with Lord Roxton.

Fortunately for Aurora, they had not to travel far before they came upon an inn, for by now Lavinia had dissolved into tears and was moaning softly into her handkerchief. Aurora was regretting for the nth time her own folly for allowing herself to be drawn into this highly imprudent venture. They should have turned back as soon as it became evident they would not catch up with the pair before nightfall. With no proper clothes, tired horses, and an inadequate carriage, it was the height of folly to go on. Only the thought of Melanie's plight had prevailed upon her better judgment and caused her to continue in pursuit.

"It must be the Red Lion," she said, pulling up. There were no lights on at the inn, but a sleepy ostler carrying a dimmed lantern came stumbling out of the house.

Aurora repeated her query. To her and Lavinia's surprise the man's reaction was vehement. "Yes, they were here, ma'am. But his lordship wouldn't stay. The chambers were not to his liking," he added in an injured tone.

Only then did Aurora realize that the man was not the ostler as she had at first supposed, but the outraged landlord himself.

"You mean they were—are stopping for the night somewhere nearby?" she asked, leaning forward eagerly.

"Aye. That's so, ma'am. But if his lordship thinks the White Pigeon has better chambers and cleaner sheets—ho, ho! As for the ale they serve there, nothing but dishwater."

"So you know where they are staying. Is this other inn far from here?" Aurora inquired.

"It's a piece down the road and then turn left. It's out of the way, it is, almost in the woods. How can the likes of a gentleman like him choose that old barn over my establishment, I'll never know."

"I'm much obliged to you," Aurora said, preparing to drive on. She sensed more than saw the man's curiosity.

"Anything I can do for you, miss?"

"No, nothing. Yet. Perhaps on our way back we shall stop here, if you say that other inn is no fit place to spend the night."

"I should say not! It's a pigsty, it is," said the affronted landlord.

Aurora thanked him again and once more prodded the tired animals into action.

"I suppose he chose that other place precisely because it is out of the way. Nobody would hear Melanie's cries for help," Aurora surmised.

"Merciful heavens!" Lavinia was outraged. "You don't mean he would try to seduce her before the wedding?"

"You know the gentleman in question better than I."

"The old rogue might be capable of that, if he were in his cups. Do you suppose he has been drinking?" Lavinia queried.

"Again I do not know. Is he in the habit of drinking to excess?"

"Of course he is. Merciful heavens! I shall have a *spasm!*"

"Not on the open road and not while I'm driving," Aurora said tightly.

Lavinia sniffed. "What a hard creature you are, Aurora. You have no sensibility at all. I think—I think it would be better when we arrive at the inn if—if you were to alight first and discover how things stand, while I remain in the carriage. I couldn't face a tragic situation, not in my present condition. You discover how things stand, explain matters to old Silverdale, if indeed it is Silverdale, then come out and apprise me of the situation."

Aurora's mouth twisted into a wry smile. Trust Lavinia to avoid any unpleasantness. Only where Lord Style was concerned was she willing to risk Lord Roxton's wrath. Were her affections for the unestimable baron deeper than either she or the earl suspected?

But Aurora had more pressing matters on her mind.

Sometime later they noticed a solitary house in the distance, with a wood stretching on its right and a pasture on the left. By the light of a few stars Aurora managed to drive the vehicle along the uneven country lane until she arrived before the completely dark and silent inn. Though she saw no post chaise in the yard, a large sign above the door depicting a white pigeon creaked in the faint breeze.

Aurora waited for a moment. No one came out to greet them. The inn remained silent and secretive. She called out sharply for the landlord. There was no response.

"They can't be here," Lavinia wailed. "I don't see a chaise anywhere."

"It might be on the other side of the house," Aurora answered. "I had better alight and knock on the door. They might be all asleep. And we must make sure if they are staying here or not."

She was on the point of climbing down when a groom staggered out of the house, yawning and scratching his head. Aurora hailed him but, impatient at his slow approach, she jumped down and stepped toward him. Immediately her nostrils were assailed by hot fumes of an unmistakably alcoholic nature. The man reeked of brandy, Aurora noted with disgust.

The man stared stupidly at her. "Your—your ladyship desires?" he mumbled.

"Is there an older gentleman and a very young miss staying at this inn? They were riding in a post-chaise-and-four."

The man nodded eagerly and waved his hand toward the house. "They're here."

Aurora heaved a deep sight of relief and returned to the carriage. "They *are* here."

"Thank God," Lavinia moaned in a hoarse voice.

"I shall go within and seek out the landlord," Aurora told her, "for that man is quite drunk and I doubt if he can even tell me what chamber Melanie occupies."

"They must all be asleep. Oh, hurry, Aurora. I am freezing with cold."

Aurora strode past the swaying groom and pushed open the rickety door. A stale, sour odor greeted her nostrils. Faugh! And Lord Silverdale would stay *here?* Only *one* circumstance would compel him to do so, she thought with misgivings.

She entered a dark chamber leading to the left, which by the feeble light streaming from the window she recognized as the taproom. It was empty. She returned to the hall and called loudly for the landlord. Lord Silverdale would not recognize her voice, even if he were awake. After hearing a muffled shout from somewhere within the inn, she returned to the taproom to await the innkeeper.

After a few moments the old door creaked open, and a tousle-headed man carrying a lighted candle appeared on the threshold.

His eyes widened when he saw Aurora. "What—what—how can I be of service, ma'am?" he said and tried to bow. He was evidently quite surprised to see her. And no wonder.

"I was given to understand that Lord Silverdale and a young lady are staying here," she said without preamble. "An old gentleman and a quite young miss. They arrived in a post chaise. They are here, aren't they?"

The man blinked, scratched his chin, then shuffled to the mantelpiece and placed the candle in a candlestick.

"Well, answer me, man. Are they here?" Aurora said sharply. Surely she and Lavinia had not come all that way on a wild goose chase.

"They are and they ain't," said the man, scratching his chin with grubby fingers.

"What do you mean, they are and they aren't?" cried Aurora. "Make sense, if you please."

"The young lady is here..."

"Then take me up to her chamber at once. I'm sorry if I have to wake her up, but it is most urgent."

"But the gentleman—"

"Bother the gentleman. If he is not here— Is he? Or if he's asleep, much the better. Show me her chamber."

"Oh, the gentleman is here right enough, but—but his name is not Silver—Silver-something. Leastways he didn't say it was. He said he was the young lady's brother."

Aurora gave a sarcastic laugh. "Of course he would say that," she began, but broke off and whirled around. From the yard came the sound of horses hoofs, and close upon it a loud scream pierced the still night air.

Lavinia! Leaving the landlord gaping, Aurora rushed outside.

The horrifying spectacle sent a chill down her spine.

Their tired horses had bolted and were dragging the carriage helter-skelter along the bumpy road. Precariously perched on top, Lavinia was trying to grab the reins to stop them.

"Oh, my God!" Aurora cried as another scream rent the air. Lavinia was leaning forward, she was overbalancing. She couldn't hold the horses.

"Aurora, help!" Lavinia screamed.

"Oh, no!" Aurora cried and ran forward even as the widow overbalanced completely, tumbled off the carriage, and lay still.

"Lavinia!" A horrified male cry sounded behind Aurora. She whirled around. In the faint starlight she beheld the pale, wide-eyed countenance of Alphonsus Fant, Baron of Style.

- 14 -

AURORA HAD NO time to consider Lord Style's presence.
She was running toward Lavinia, but as fast as she was, the
baron outdistanced her. She would never have believed he
could run so swiftly. By the time she had arrived beside the
fallen widow, the baron was kneeling on the ground, cradling her head in his lap and crying out piteously, "Lavinia,
Vinny! Speak to me. Oh, Vinny, speak to me! Say you are
not dead."

Aurora dropped onto her knees beside them and felt
Lavinia's pulse. "She is alive, but obviously unconscious."

Lord Style lifted wild eyes to Aurora. "We must fetch
a doctor immediately." Then, bending down again: "Lavinia, Vinny."

The widow moaned, and her eyelids fluttered.

"She is alive, she is coming round!" the baron cried
joyously, but as Lavinia's head lolled back, he added,
"She—she isn't—?"

Her hand on Lavinia's pulse, Aurora said evenly, "No,
she has merely swooned again. She must be in pain. We
must carry her to bed. But carefully."

"Yes, of course." Before Aurora's astonished gaze, Lord

Style struggled to his feet, lifted Lady Lanville tenderly in his arms, and began to walk with her toward the inn.

If he wasn't genuinely in love with her, she had never seen a man in love before, thought Aurora. Why the deuce did Lord Roxton try to keep them apart if such was the case?

At the entrance to the inn, the landlord and the groom stood staring, mouths agape.

"You idiot! You imbecile!" the baron rounded on the groom. "How *could* you have made the horses bolt with the lady in the carriage?"

"I—I was just following your lordship's orders," the young man muttered.

"You dolt! You drunken, witless blackguard! Haven't you any brains in your stupid head? Has the brandy melted your reason?"

Aurora touched his arm. "My lord, it is imperative to attend to Lady Lanville's hurts with all possible speed."

"Oh, yes. To be sure. You"—he turned to the inn-keeper—"go and fetch a doctor—if one can be found in this godforsaken place. And go yourself! As for you"—he turned to the groom—"I shall deal with you later!" So grim was his tone, so full of suppressed fury and hatred, that Aurora was persuaded that if his lordship's hands had been free, it would have fared ill with the hapless groom. But to make the horses bolt deliberately? What did it all signify?

Lavinia moaned. Immediately the baron turned to her. "Yes, my love. We shall make you better in a trice. Miss Marshingham, pray call the landlady, Mrs. Mulligan, and desire her to fetch water and some linen and—and hartshorn and vinegar and all that is needed."

"Certainly, I—"

"I'll take her to Melanie's chamber."

A stifled cry made them look up. Melanie, holding onto the banister with one hand and carrying a candle in the other, was staring at them, her eyes enormous in her pale face.

"Lady Lanville! Miss Marshingham! What has occurred? And where—where is Lord Albert? Oh—"

"Don't stand there gawking, girl! Light the way up the stairs," commanded the baron, but Melanie remained frozen with horror.

Aurora gently removed the candle from her fingers and turned her around. "Come, we must do all we can to help Lady Lanville."

Melanie gulped. "Is she—is she . . . ?"

"No, she isn't; but she might get worse if she doesn't receive immediate help." Aurora prodded the shaking girl up the stairs, while the baron followed with his burden.

He placed Lavinia on Melanie's bed. The widow was moaning feebly, but her eyes remained closed. The baron knelt beside the bed and began chafing her hands while murmuring tender endearments and entreaties, urging her to open her eyes.

Aurora cast one glance at the shaking and sobbing Melanie huddled by the fireplace and decided with a shrug that she could not tend both ladies at once. She proceeded to light a lamp that she had found on the mantelpiece and by its illumination examined her cousin's hurts. There was a bruise on her cheek and a lump the size of a hen's egg on her head. A concussion! Aurora thought with dismay. Next she examined Lavinia's arms and then, disregarding all propriety, lifted the hem of her skirts to examine her legs. One was swollen and, to Aurora's experienced eyes, appeared to be broken.

"Melanie, have you a vinaigrette with you?" Aurora turned to the girl. "Melanie!" She had to shake the sobbing damsel and repeat her request before the frightened Melanie could respond.

"In m-my reticule," she stammered.

Aurora found the vinaigrette and placed it in the baron's hand. "Wave it under her nose while I'll see about the water," she said, and went off in search of the innkeeper's wife.

The next hour was a busy and trying one for Aurora, what with washing the widow's hurts and attempting to revive her, giving commands to the help, and trying to prevent Melanie from having hysterics. Lavinia regained consciousness several times during Aurora's ministrations, but each time she swooned again.

Only once did she speak, and that was to the baron. When she regained consciousness for the first time and caught sight of him, she gasped out, "Alphonsus, pray do not be vexed . . . with me. I-I did it for the best."

The baron, delighted she was speaking to him once more, assured her fervently, "How can I ever be vexed with you, Vinny? I love you."

And then Lavinia's eyes filled with tears and she swooned again. The baron cursed, bit his lip, and cursed some more.

At last the doctor came and, to Aurora's relief, dosed Melanie Fant with laudanum. She went to sleep on the truckle bed set up in the room. Then the doctor examined Lavinia. He confirmed Aurora's surmise. The widow had broken a leg, besides numerous cuts and bruises, and possibly a concussion. She needed the leg in a splint and to be kept as quiet as possible. The doctor, perceiving that the inn was hardly a fit place for an invalid gentlewoman, reluctantly consented to allow the baron to drive Lady Lanville home in his post chaise. Finally, after promising to come in the morning to personally supervise the handling of her ladyship into the chaise and providing some drops and instructions on how to care for her, the doctor departed, leaving the baron and Aurora to watch over the widow.

Aurora ordered tea and tried to coax Lord Style to bed. "You cannot help her now. Very likely she will not wake before morning. The doctor has made her comfortable, and I am persuaded she will pass a quiet night. There is no need for you to sit up with her. I shall ask Mrs. Mulligan to set up another truckle for me here and I shall keep watch."

The baron raised red-rimmed eyes. "Do you really think she will be restored to health?" he murmured, groaning. "She will recover?"

"Of course she will," Aurora assured him. "I've desired Mrs. Mulligan to bring us some tea and—"

"Devil take tea! Oh, I beg your pardon. But if I have to drink, it had better be something stronger."

"I rather think *not*. You need to have your wits about you, my lord."

The baron sighed. "Yes, you are in the right of it." He pushed his hand distractedly through his hair, his gaze on Lavinia.

At that moment, Baron Style, that elegant tulip, presented an extraordinary appearance. His hair was disheveled, his countenance haggard and pale, his pale-yellow pantaloons dirty, and his Hessian boots spattered with mud. His coat hung open, and his pink-and-green striped waistcoat sported a large tear. His neckcloth was awry, and his stiffly starched shirt collar had wilted. Aurora had never seen him in such a disorderly condition. It spoke volumes for the state of his mind that he had remained completely unaware of it.

Mrs. Mulligan entered carrying a tray with a teapot, chipped cups and saucers, and some scones. After she had left and Aurora had poured the tea, she remarked critically as she eyed with disfavor the not prepossessing crockery, "Why in the world did he choose this of all places? I daresay those cups haven't been washed properly for at least a week. But I suppose it would be useless to demand others."

The baron took the cup from her hands and began to sip his tea absently.

"This place is shockingly dirty," Aurora continued. "And that slovenly woman who runs it and that rascal of a landlord—I don't see how Lord Silverdale came to choose this place. Unless he intended some—some particular mischief. I hope you have managed to prevent him. What did happen to him?"

The baron raised tired eyes to her face. "Huh? Silverdale? He's got nothing to do with it. I chose this place."

"What?"

"I own it is shockingly shabby, but it is out of the way, and that rascally innkeeper stands in my debt. I should have known they would make a botch of it, though," he added bitterly.

"Make a botch of it? Lord Style, I'm afraid I don't understand."

"No. And neither do I," he said abruptly, placing the cup and saucer on the table so hard that it rattled. "How came you and Lavinia to be here at this hour? Why isn't Albert here? I made sure he would fly to Melanie's rescue."

"Lord Style, you knew of the missive your sister left for the viscount!"

"Knew of it? Of course I knew of it! I told her to write it."

"You told her to—to—" Aurora was bereft of speech.

"Oh, this is beyond anything! You mean it was all a trick, just as Lavinia suspected?"

The baron seemed faintly interested. "No? Did she, though! By Jove, I always said she knew me better than anyone else. But if she suspected the elopement was a hoax, why in thunder is she here now? What possessed her to run after Melanie, and how did she come to know of the elopement?"

"She—she—We paid a call on the viscount. Her ladyship wished to have some word with him in private, but he was from home so she decided to wait. She observed a billet on the mantelpiece, from your sister, and picked it up and it wasn't perfectly sealed and . . ."

"She read it. Well, she always liked snooping," Lord Style said dispassionately. "But why the deuce did she—"

"She was afraid what would happen if the viscount were to go after your sister and Lord Silverdale," Aurora explained.

"Damn her for her meddling! No, not damn." His gaze returned to Lavinia's pale face. "But I wish for once she had left things as they were. That was precisely what I wanted—what she was trying to avoid. I wished Albert to feel he had to act chivalrous toward Melanie."

"And when he came here and found out there was no elopement?"

"I trusted Melanie to keep him here for the night. At least I hoped that ninny would. To make sure, I told that drunken groom to make Albert's horses bolt. That would have made it impossible for him to drive Melanie back to London that night. All I needed was Melanie and Albert to spend one night under one roof. Then he would have been honor bound to marry her, and Roxton could not have prevented it."

"Of all the infamous, scandalous, outrageous tricks, this is the worst!" Aurora jumped up and took a turn about the room. "Lord Style, you are a scoundrel!"

The baron bared his teeth in the unpleasant grin she remembered. "Sometimes, regrettably, one is forced to adopt deplorable means to achieve one's ends. I wanted those estates back. Here was a rare opportunity of achieving that, and Roxton was going to upset it all, as always. So Albert isn't even aware of what transpired?"

"No. And neither is anyone else. They must be quite frantic at Berkely Square, for no one knows where we are. Lady Lanville decided to chase after the eloping pair on the spur of the moment, and she wanted us to start off at once so as to return to London before nightfall. But she stopped for rest at every other postinghouse and—"

The baron nodded. "No need to tell *me*. I can conceive the rest. But what a shatterbrained thing to do, even for her—to start out without proper preparations and an escort!" He gave Aurora a rueful smile. "You must have had the devil of a time with her. Oh, I *beg* your pardon."

"Not at all. And you are right. I had," Aurora agreed heartily. But she was astounded. The baron seemed to have few illusions about his inamorata. Yet he still loved her.

"I have a notion, Lord Style, that you should have married Lavinia. She was right when she said you understand her perfectly. You do. I am sure you are just the right husband for her. And if anyone can stop her from having vapors and hysterics, it is you."

"She don't play *me* any of her tricks," said the baron.

Oh, it would be all too ridiculous—if it weren't so outrageous, Aurora decided. The baron had behaved very badly. Yet . . . perhaps if Lord Roxton had been a trifle more reasonable toward him, all this wouldn't have happened. Aurora longed to ask the baron why Lord Roxton disliked him so excessively, but of course she dared not do so. Just because the earl's brother and the baron had been drinking together on the night of the brother's accident did not seem to her to be reason enough for the earl's hatred.

The baron became lost in thought for a moment, but presently he said, speaking more to himself than to her, "Yes, I should have married her. I know how to handle her; Will didn't. She played him a merry hell, and he stood it all, poor chap. I don't think he had the least notion what he was letting himself in for when he married her. Of course he dazzled her with his manners and his looks—that could not be denied. Though in those days I wasn't bad looking myself. But she was bound to marry him. The money."

"I don't think such considerations should have swayed Lady Lanville," Aurora said quickly.

"Huh? Oh. I beg your pardon. I shouldn't be talking to you about this. Oh, what's the odds. You know Lavinia and by now you think you know me pretty well too." He winked at her in a roguish way. The man was impossible! He was not at all ashamed of what he had done. On the other hand, he did not seem offended or hurt at her having a poor opinion of him. One could not help but like him for that, Aurora admitted reluctantly. For the first time she began to understand Lavinia's infatuation with the baron.

"As for Lavinia's reason for throwing me over—" His face grew somber again and he cast an anxious glance at the widow. "No, no, you do her an injustice. She actually fancied herself in love with Will. Of course she never was. Found his family stifling. Devilish proper and high in the instep, all the Lanvilles except perhaps Will. But he tried to conform. Poor chap. I'm sorry he's dead, but—" He shook his head. "A bad marriage can be hell on earth.

"But I must beg your pardon, Miss Marshingham" the baron continued. "Here I am prosing on like a veritable gabster, or worse, one of those gossipy tabbies. My worry for Lavinia has loosened my tongue."

"I do think you ought to get some rest, Lord Style."

"No. I wish to remain here, beside her."

"Just as you please; but there isn't another decent chamber where I can spend the night, and I think your lordship would be well advised to change your clothes."

"What? Oh? The devil!" He swore and shuddered as for the first time he became aware of the state of his attire. "I look like a gypsy. My best pantaloons! My Hessians! And I don't have my valet with me," the baron moaned. "Damnation, there is actually a hole in my waistcoat! Miss Marshingham, I must beg you a thousand pardons for remaining before you in such a deplorable state. I am *most* grateful to you for bringing it to my attention."

He cast another worried glance at the widow, but it was evident that his thoughts were a great deal diverted by the damage his clothes had sustained. He turned to stare at Aurora. "It is a pity you think so ill of me because of this adventure. Alas, I meant nobody any harm, least of all Lavinia. You will look after her, won't you, Miss Marshingham?"

"Of course I will," she assured him

"And promise to call me if—if she worsens or—or if she wakes and calls for me."

"Yes, yes. I shall do all that is required and proper."

"I am much obliged to you. You know, I think you have a very good heart, Miss Marshingham. Not many females would tolerate Lavinia's whims."

"To own the truth, I have wished her to the devil many times, but I don't want her to come to any harm. And don't look so surprised at my using improper language. According to Lord Roxton, I'm past praying for."

"I wouldn't worry overmuch about that," the baron said soothingly. "I think he likes you a great deal."

"What? No, no. You must be mistaken. He thinks I'm the worst possible jade."

"He probably thinks that too. That's why it makes him so devilish cross. Roxton ain't a bad sort really, just very high in the instep and inclined to judge all persons according to his high standards of propriety. Silly thing to do, for all people can't be the same. But there, that's Lord Roxton for you. Don't tease yourself on his account. He'll come around." Lord Style rose ponderously and, after glancing at Lavinia once more, gave Aurora a deep bow, bid her good night, and departed, grumbling under his breath and inspecting a smudge on his coat sleeve through his quizzing glass.

After he had gone, Aurora pondered Lord Style's astonishing statement. He must be mistaken, of course. Lord Roxton couldn't possible like her. She shook her head. No matter. She wouldn't have much more to do with the earl, for as soon as she returned to London, she would take the first Mail back to Yorkshire. And that would be that.

But the thought of returning home was a depressing one. She had failed to establish herself in a position so as to provide for her sisters. Perhaps she really ought to wait until after the grand duchess's ball. Perhaps the widow would find her a post after all. But Lavinia was not likely to attend any balls in the near future.

- *15* -

AURORA WAKENED TO the insistent calling of her name.
Blinking sleep away from her eyes, at first she did not
realize where she was. But as soon as she saw Bellman,
Lady Lanville's personal maid, she recollected. She was
back in her chamber in Berkeley Square. She sat up with
a jerk. "Is her ladyship worse?" she asked.

"No, not yet. But I very much fear what may happen.
Lord Style is with her."

"What?" Aurora exclaimed. "I told him particularly not
to come calling here unless I sent word to him."

"Well, he has come. He won't upset her ladyship, but
if Lord Roxton pays her a visit, there will be a rare to-do.
And that—that *creature*, begging your pardon, miss"—she
sniffed—"Lord Style's sister, has woken up and has the
fidgets. She's roaming about the house insisting on seeing
Lady Lanville."

"Oh, dear. I was going to restore her to Lord Style myself
as soon as she was up. I would have done so yesterday, but
she was still in such a poor state."

"Just so, miss." Bellman nodded.

"What is the time?" inquired Aurora.

"It's past ten o'clock, miss."

"Oh, great heavens! I have overslept. I shall dress immediately and send Lord Style on his way. Meanwhile do what you can to speed his departure. You are positive Lady Lanville is not worse?" Aurora asked again.

"No. If anything she is a trifle better," Bellman reassured her.

"Thank heavens for that. I shall be with her directly. Thank you, Bellman."

The woman curtsied and withdrew.

Aurora pulled at the bell rope and jumped out of bed. She shouldn't have allowed herself to oversleep, but she really couldn't have contrived to get up early. The night before, at that dreadful inn, she hadn't slept a wink, for Lavinia was very restless. The next day, after they had all arrived at Berkeley Square in Lord Style's chaise, she had had her hands full helping to make Lavinia comfortable in her bedchamber, sending out for doctors, and tending to Melanie's hysterics. The widow was in a pitiable state, the jolting of the coach not having helped matters. But fortunately the doctors were of the opinion that no lasting damage was done, and she should recover uneventfully. Then there were the children to be looked after, for they had become upset with all the strange goings-on and couldn't be kept in the nursery. And as Nurse was taken with a strong fit of palpitations, and the other servants were powerless to control the youngsters, Aurora had to take a hand herself. She was kept busy running from the sickroom to the nursery and back again, and in between she had to drop in to soothe Melanie, who was moaning and weeping in her bedchamber.

After having at last bedded the children and seen them and Melanie drift into a deep sleep, it had been quite late at night that Aurora, tired and heavy-lidded herself, had crawled between the sheets. She had fallen asleep and slept the night through.

It did not take Aurora long to wash and dress, and without waiting for breakfast, she rushed to the widow's bedchamber.

Lady Lanville, in a fetching lace cap and frilled pink nightgown, was reposing on her bed, propped up on several pillows, while Lord Style was sitting on a chair beside the

bed holding one of her slim hands in his own. He appeared
his usual resplendent self in pale-biscuit pantaloons and
polished Hessians. His lilac coat molded his shoulders,
and his shirt collars once more stayed up proudly, starched
and straight. Fob, seal, quizzing glass—everything was in
its proper place. But the expression on his countenance was
not that of a vacuous dandy. His eyes gazed with deep
affection at the widow, while Lavinia stared soulfully back
into his eyes.

Aurora gave a little cough.

The widow started and would have withdrawn her hand,
but the baron merely pressed it tighter, while he turned
toward Aurora. "Ah, good morning, Miss Marshingham.
I trust you have slept well. You look particularly radiant
this morning." He was going to rise, but Aurora waved him
back.

The widow pouted. "I wish you had knocked, Aurora,"
she said pettishly. "Can't you see I desire to be private with
his lordship?"

"I am glad you are feeling so much better as to indulge
in conversation with Lord Style, but I have come to beg him
to leave. It was most imprudent of you to have come here,
Lord Style. We have managed to avoid Lord Roxton's censure only because he was out of town. But he will be back
today; for all we know, he is back already. It won't do at
all for him to find you here."

"Let him find Alphonsus," Lavinia sulked. "I am tired
of going in terror of him all my days."

"Nevertheless, you are in too weak a state to provoke
a scene of the sort that cannot but be injurious to your
nerves."

"I want Alphonsus to stay," fretted the widow.

The baron sighed. "I'm afraid Miss Marshingham is in
the right of it, my love. I should go. I must beg your pardon,
Miss Marshingham, for not waiting for your note. But I was
that concerned about Lady Lanville; my worry overcame
my prudence. No, indeed, we can't have Roxton fly into
one of his rages now. I suppose I better collect Melanie
while I'm here. I understand she is up."

"Yes, she is," Aurora confirmed. "And I hate to throw

her out thus, Lord Style, but *you* understand. It isn't only that Lord Roxton might object to her presence here. It's well—She isn't—isn't exactly—"

"Bright," the baron supplied bluntly. "And wouldn't know how to hold her tongue. Not that the servants' hall isn't full of gossip."

"But they don't know the whole truth. They only surmise, whereas Melanie—"

Lady Lanville's other hand flew to her bosom. "Oh, yes. It would be *disastrous* were she to reveal the whole truth to Roxton. Alphonsus, you *must* take her away. Tiresome girl. But you will come back, won't you? Pray leave us alone for a few moments, Aurora, so that he can take proper leave of me," Lavinia begged.

"Kiss you, you mean. Oh, very well. But pray make haste, for it would not do—"

Aurora was interrupted by a soft knock on the door. Hatchetfaced Bellman appeared on the threshold, great perturbation mirrored on her severe countenance. She shut the door furtively behind her.

"Your lordship best escape. Lord Roxton is belowstairs!"

"Oh, my Lord!" shrieked Lavinia, grasping the baron agitatedly by his coat sleeve. "You must go! You must flee immediately!"

Lord Style gently disengaged her clutching fingers. "Don't put yourself in a taking, my love. It is only natural that I should rush to your bedside the minute I discovered that—"

"Your lordship doesn't know the *half* of it." Bellman paused dramatically for a second. "That little ninny—begging your pardon, your lordship—your lordship's sister, has blurted out the *whole* story."

"What! Oh, I *am* going to have a spasm," Lavinia cried and fell back on the pillows, deadly white. Even the baron's face paled considerably.

"How came she to tell it?" started Aurora.

"I forgot to say. The Viscount Deberough entered almost on the heels of the earl. They both went to the yellow salon. Miss Fant was there. The minute she clapped eyes on the viscount, she melted and started to pour out the whole story to him, with Lord Roxton there soaking up everything. Now she is in hysterics, and the viscount is comforting her. And Lord Roxton will be up here any moment."

An imperative knock on the door confirmed her words. Then the door burst open and the earl, booted, spurred, and looking like a thundercloud, entered the chamber.

Lavinia moaned faintly and closed her eyes, while the baron, pale but composed, rose to his feet.

"*So*. You are determined to be the ruin of our family, are you, Style," the earl said grimly. "Don't try to deny it, for I know the whole story. And you, ma'am"—he turned to Aurora in concentrated fury—"you, ma'am, aided and abetted him in this despicable plot. I could never fathom how you ever came to be his light-o'-love, but by God, I see now that you two deserve each other."

"Roxton, you forget yourself. You are insulting Miss Marshingham and accusing her quite unjustly," the baron exclaimed.

Lavinia opened one eye. "Indeed, it is so," she moaned. "Aurora has not the faintest notion...As for being Alphonsus's—No, how *can* you suggest—"

"Your language, Roxton, is more suited to the stables than to a lady's ears," continued the baron.

"Quiet, both of you. I shall have no more lies and prevarications. And no more interference from you, Style. Once and for all I shall destroy your evil influence upon my family. You have gone one step too far, and you shall give me satisfaction now for all the insults and hurt you have inflicted upon our name."

The baron's countenance turned ashen, but he said in a tolerably steady voice, "Talk about Cheltenham tragedies—"

"No, no, Alphonsus!" interrupted the widow, her eyes round with horror. "He means to call you out! You must *not* accept his challenge. You *mustn't!*"

"Don't worry yourself, my love. Of course I shan't meet him. I will not fight any duel."

"Oh, yes, you shall. I will make sure once and for all that you shall never dare to call her your love again." And with one quick stride the earl was beside the baron and struck him full across the cheek with his glove. "Now, shall you give me satisfaction?"

The baron swayed a little under the impact of the blow, while Lavinia uttered a hysterical cry and began to thrash about. But Lord Style's face was now turning purple. "By God, I *have* had enough of your high and mighty ways, Roxton! Yes, I shall give you all the satisfaction you desire. I shall meet you when and where you please. And you can choose the weapons. *I* have had enough of *you* and your interfering ways, enough of your badgering Lavinia and standing in my way—"

"Alphonsus, are you out of your mind?" Lavinia was beside herself. "He will kill you. He is a deadly shot, and you know it."

The baron laughed, a reckless, bitter laugh. "Aye, and if he kills me, what's the odds? At least he will have appeased his—his fustian thirst for revenge. And you shall not be troubled by my presence any more."

"But I *do* want to be troubled, I want to!" the widow shouted and fell into a strong fit of the vapors, while the baron, his head held high, strode out of the chamber.

"I think you are abominable and unnecessarily cruel," Aurora flared at the earl. "Now look at what you have done. Lady Lanville had but yesterday sustained a severe injury to her head and a broken leg, besides numerous cuts and bruises. She is quite ill, and I mean *really* ill, and you have caused her to have one of her worst spasms."

"Pray leave this chamber at once, your lordship," Bellman also snapped at the earl, "or my lady will be much worse. Miss Marshingham, pray desire Stobbins to fetch the doctor immediately."

The earl stood nonplussed for a moment, the anger and hate slowly draining from his face. At last he said, "I wasn't aware—at least Melanie didn't say Lady Lanville was seriously ill."

"That little ninny!" Bellman snorted. "You trust *her* to tell you a story you can make heads or tails of. I beg your lordship to withdraw. Miss Marshingham—"

"Yes, yes, directly."

"Miss Marshingham." The earl opened the door and let Aurora precede him out of the room, casting a last worried glance at Lavinia. Aurora stalked past him, her head held high, her cheeks aflame with mortification at having been called names in front of the widow and Lord Style, and above all in front of Bellman.

"Miss Marshingham—" the earl began once more, after the door had closed behind them.

Aurora ignored him completely and increased her pace. The earl caught up with her, grabbed her by the arm, and twisted it. "Miss Marshingham, I desire to have speech with you."

Aurora tossed her head. "But I do not. Pray let me go."

The earl released her arm. "Don't be an idiot," he snapped. "You must understand my position. I but arrive in Mount Street and am met with the intelligence that Lavinia is prostrated and that that scoundrel and his sister are once more making themselves at home in my brother's house. And when I rush here, I come upon a hysterical female who mumbles out a disjointed tale of a make-believe Gretna Green elopement arranged by *her* brother to entrap *my* brother into marriage with her. It is true, it was hard to make sense out of what she was babbling about, but I thought I understood enough. There was a trap set for Albert, wasn't there?"

"Yes. Unfortunately there was."

The earl's hands clenched at his sides. "Was Lavinia aware of it?"

"No. In the process of trying to mend matters, she was hurt."

"Surely Style couldn't have struck her. Melanie babbled something about a runaway carriage."

"Yes. Lady Lanville fell out of the phaeton when her horses bolted."

"How? How did that happen? No, never mind, it doesn't signify now. And your own involvement in the matter, Miss Marshingham?"

Aurora shot him a fiery glance out of her blazing eyes. "You may make of it what you choose, my lord. It is of supreme indifference to me."

Once more his iron grip closed about her arm. "But it is not of indifference to me," he said, gritting his teeth.

"I fail to see the reason for it. Surely as Lord Style's 'light-o'-love' I can be capable of anything that is most vile. Pray release me, my lord."

But the grip only tightened. "Are you his light-o'-love then?" he cried, and there was a strange ring to his voice.

"I fail to see why that should interest you either. As soon as her ladyship is on the mend and the nurse recovered, I shall remove myself from Berkeley Square. I would go tomorrow, but I collect both Lavinia and the children need me."

"No. You shall not take care of the children," thundered the earl, but at the same time he let go her arm.

Aurora made him a mocking curtsy. "What? Afraid that I shall contaminate them with my evil ways? Even were I capable of that and so inclined, they are too young yet to be corrupted. But set your mind at ease. Find someone in this household who is able to look after them and I shall gladly leave this house tomorrow. No, tonight!"

"And where will you go tonight? To his lodgings? You jade—" He was gripping her by the arm once more.

"Again, my lord, that is my affair. My life is no concern of yours. Pray let me go. You are hurting my arm."

"I would like to hurt more than your arm. I would like to wring your neck," he cried but released her. "And you are mistaken in thinking your life is no concern of mine. It *must* be my concern. I have *made* it my concern. Or have you forgotten that it is I who am responsible for your present deplorable circumstances? If I had not been remiss in my promises, you, I believe, would not have been reduced to consorting with the likes of Style. I trust that you did not make his acquaintance while Lord Treeton was still alive. He would not have countenanced that."

The utter contempt in his voice stung Aurora into speaking out in the baron's defense. "Perhaps, my lord, my father would not have held so prejudiced an opinion of Lord Style as you do. He is not a model of propriety, to be sure, but I cannot believe him a monster."

"Then you are an imbecile. Or worse, you are in love with the man."

"And you, my lord, are as ill mannered as you are full of prejudice. Even the commonest civility would have compelled you to temper your expressions. But you have no consideration of another person's feelings. Which leads me to wonder what in heaven's name has possessed you to exhibit such concern in my life. Can it possibly be that you are suffering from a guilty conscience? I can hardly believe you possess one, judging by the callous way you treat others."

"I will not stand here and be sermonized at by you," the earl ground through his teeth.

"No, my lord? Then pray let me pass. I shall be very happy to remove myself from your presence."

"No." The earl detained her. "I must talk to you. Whatever you may think of me—and whatever I think of you— the fact remains that your affairs are in a sad state, and I must help you settle them. No, I realize it is of no use speaking of it now. You are much too overwrought. But when you have had time to reflect on the matter and to cool that temper of yours—"

"Hah! *You* speak of tempers!"

"When you have had time to reflect," repeated the earl, disregarding her exclamation, "you shall come to realize that only with my help can you contrive to achieve that position which is rightfully yours. And if you do not think of yourself, think of your sisters. Consider their future. But we'll talk no more of that at present. Tell me, how is Lavinia? Has a competent surgeon been sent for? Dr. Babcock is a good man but hardly the person to call in a serious emergency."

"We had three doctors to see her." Aurora tried to answer him civilly. "Dr. Babcock and two others. Lord Style assured me they were the best, but I did not catch their names. As for Lady Lanville, she was a little stouter this morning; but I'm afraid your—your outrageous behavior has set her quite back. I shall have to explain the whole to Dr. Babcock. I'll send a note round to him, for we are to call him first and—"

"No need to send a note. I shall fetch him myself. At once."

Aurora made him another mock curtsy. "How noble and considerate of you, my lord!"

His color changed. He studied her thoughtfully for a moment. "You have a pretty poor notion of my character."

"Possibly mine is a shade better than yours is of me."

"Touché!" admitted the earl. He sighed and suddenly

passed his hand wearily across his brow. "I wish I knew how to untangle this coil. I shall have the devil's own time to drag that weeping willow from Albert's side. Hell and damnation!" he suddenly swore. "Why did you have to throw the two of them together!"

"For reasons that must always elude your lordship."

"What reasons? I fail to see . . ." The earl was confused.

"Precisely. And since you—"

"He is my brother. What right have you to meddle in my and his affairs?" he interrupted.

Aurora was suddenly very tired. Tears welled up under her eyelids. "Because Melanie is in love with him, has been in love with him for years, and because I—I thought a silly and compliant wife would be exactly the sort of female he would be comfortable with. And he seemed quite smitten with her too. If it turns out to be a lasting passion, nothing, I venture to say, would be better. For to have him fall in and out of love with a whole lot of ineligible females is not at all the thing. One of them just might contrive to force him to the altar. He isn't very . . . well, he can be easily swayed by a pretty and shrewd woman."

The earl stared at her oddly for a moment, then said, as if much struck by the idea, "You may be in the right of it. If only she were anyone other than Style's sister."

"Why do you hate Lord Style so much, my lord?" Aurora could not help asking.

The earl stiffened. "I do not discuss my private affairs with anyone."

Aurora shrugged. "It is no concern of mine. But if I were you, I would examine my motives closely and take another hard look at the baron."

"You dare tell me what to do!"

"Not telling, merely suggesting," Aurora said calmly. "And only because I feel there is real affection between him and Lady Lanville. Trying to keep them apart is patently wrong. And cruel. But then cruelty seems to be your second nature, my lord. Some guardian you shall turn out to be for your niece and nephew! I pity them when they grow older and are obliged to submit to your fits of temper."

"You are very harsh, ma'am," the earl returned. "I assure

you I am not out of reason cross with anybody, as a rule. Least of all with my brother's children."

"You cared for him a great deal, didn't you?" Aurora asked quietly.

"Yes. I—I was his and Albert's guardian, but I was closer to Will," the earl answered. "I took care of them when our father died. I should have watched over him better. I should have prevented his marriage to Lavinia. I do not intend to make the same mistake with Albert."

"Melanie is not Lady Lanville. Lady Lanville has a strong selfish streak in her, while Melanie is just weak and silly. But she is quite good-hearted."

"A scared rabbit."

"It is not to be wondered at. Your demeanor, my lord, would scare many a tenderly nurtured damsel."

The earl bared his teeth. "But not you?"

"I am hardly a tender, hothouse flower," Aurora responded. "Nor am I just out of the schoolroom. Besides, 'jades' and 'lights-o'-love' are known for their lack of sensibility, aren't they?" And as he was looking like a black cloud once more, she added, "Good day, my lord," and made good her escape before he could think up a rejoinder biting enough to satisfy his ire.

That odious man! She would be very happy to see the last of him, thought Aurora, yet perversely she could not find any satisfaction in the thought. She did not go to the yellow salon but went directly to her chamber. Let his lordship deal with Melanie and the viscount as he saw fit. She felt a little sorry for Melanie but was persuaded Lord Albert would not let his brother bully her too much. At any rate, Aurora was determined not to have anything more to do with the lot of them. She resumed her packing, working feverishly while blinking back tears from time to time.

She could not fathom why her heart should be so heavy at the thought of leaving Berkeley Square. In her short sojourn there she had known only humiliation and trouble. And yet... She sighed impatiently and continued.

She had been thus engaged for some moments when suddenly she heard a soft tapping on the door. Aurora bade the caller to enter, and the door opened to admit Lady Lanville's personal maid.

Aurora, feeling a trifle guilty and apprehensive, asked sharply, "What is it, Bellman?"

"I have contrived to calm Lady Lanville down somewhat, but I am worried. She ought to have the doctor look in on her."

"Lord Roxton offered to fetch Dr. Babcock at once. Is there anything I can do now?"

"Her ladyship desires to have a word with you. She is overwrought at the impending duel. Oh, whatever could have possessed Lord Style to accept his lordship's challenge?"

"I don't think he could very well have refused, not with all of us present and him being slapped in the face. His honor was touched too much for him not to accept. He could not allow himself to be branded a coward in front of all of us," Aurora explained.

"Better a live coward than a dead hero," Bellman said tartly. "And what his death would do to her ladyship, I shudder to think! I am not particularly fond of his lordship or his ways, but I've been in Lady Lanville's service these many years, and I do not wish to see her ladyship hurt."

"Neither do I, but I fail to see what I can do," Aurora said as she followed Bellman out of the room.

- *16* -

AURORA WAS SHOCKED at the pallor of Lavinia's face. Even right after the accident she had not looked so wan and ghastly pale. She was clutching the vinaigrette in her hand, and her eyes were closed. Upon Aurora's entering, however, she opened them and gave a feeble cry of relief.

"Oh, Aurora, I knew I could depend upon you," she uttered in a weak voice. "You must stop them. They must not meet."

Cold dismay struck Aurora's heart. What could she do? How could she stop them?

She approached the bed. "I would do anything to prevent this duel. But what can I do?" Suddenly she brightened. "I know, I can lodge a complaint with the magistrate."

But at this the widow grew more agitated. "No, no. On no account must they be arrested. We cannot have the law brought into this. Think of the *scandal!*" She gave a weak but dramatic shudder. "Nothing must leak out to the outside world."

"If they meet, things are bound to leak out."

"But they mustn't meet, they mustn't!" Lavinia cried in a tone of urgency and despair. "You must stop them, Aurora. Go to Roxton and beg him to withdraw his challenge."

135

"What? Beg something of Lord Roxton! Nothing on earth could induce me to beg anything of him. Besides, what good would it do, even were I to go on my knees before him? Do you think he would pay any heed to anything *I* say? It would only set his back up even more."

The widow moaned in anguish. "But they *must* be stopped. Someone must do something."

"How about Lord Albert? Can't he do anything? *Him* I could ask."

"It is of no use." The widow wept. "I have asked him already. Alphonsus took Melanie away. He almost had to drag her by force from Albert's side. Albert came up to see how I was, and I told him about the duel. He won't do anything. Men are so stupid. 'One can't interfere in an affair of honor.' Bah! They make me sick!"

She closed her eyes and lay exhausted for a moment. After a while, just as Aurora was about to tiptoe out of the room, Lavinia's eyelids fluttered open and she called her back.

"Aurora, Aurora, go to Alphonsus. Explain to him that I—that I cannot bear the thought of losing him, that he must not meet Roxton. I venture to say he would not have accepted this challenge were he not in such an agitated state of mind and—and with all of you present too. But now that he has had time to think on it, he will see reason."

Aurora sighed. She foresaw only trouble with this fresh intervention on her part, but she could hardly refuse this request. Besides, the baron, not very courageous by nature, might not need much persuading.

Bellman, who had gone to stand by the window, turned around abruptly. "His lordship's curricle. He has Dr. Babcock with him."

The widow half rose from her pillows. "You must go now. He—Roxton will stay here, I am persuaded, to discover what Dr. Babcock has to say about my condition. I shall keep the doctor occupied as long as possible, so as to keep Roxton here. Go now. Roxton must not know, he must not—"

"But why go now? Wouldn't it be better to leave after the doctor and Lord Roxton have departed?" Aurora asked.

"We cannot be sure when he is to meet Alphonsus," Lavinia replied. "He might wish to do it now. I have never seen him in such a black rage before. He wants to murder him. You must stop him. Go now. You can say that you have to buy some smelling salts for me. Only go."

"If I may make so bold as to suggest, miss, it might be the only way out of this dreadful fix," added Bellman.

"Oh, very well. I shall go at once," Aurora agreed.

Lady Lanville sank back on her pillows and closed her eyes. Aurora let herself out of the room quietly.

On the landing she met Lord Roxton and the doctor coming up. The earl's face wore an anxious look. "How is she?" he asked Aurora.

"She is quieter now but dreadfully pale. Dr. Babcock, she wasn't this pale right after the accident. And she is even too weak for hysterics."

The doctor cast a reproachful glance at the earl but said nothing. Aurora entered her own chamber. Not wasting any time, she threw on her blue hooded cloak, grabbed her reticule, making sure she had enough money with her to pay off a hackney, and tiptoed hurriedly down the stairs. She met no one on her way down, but she breathed a sigh of relief as she let herself out of the house. Fortunately she was able to obtain a carriage almost instantly, and a short time later she was knocking on the door of Lord Style's lodgings.

A thin man with narrow, uneasy eyes and dressed in the livery of a valet answered her knock, raising his brows at the sight of an unaccompanied lady but inquiring politely how he could be of service.

"Inform Lord Style that I must see him at once," commanded Aurora.

The valet bowed. "Pray be so good as to step into the parlor, ma'am. Who shall I say is calling?"

"Miss Marshingham. And make haste."

"Very good, miss."

The valet ushered her into the parlor and withdrew. A few moments later the baron, his expression alarmed, hurried into the room.

"Lavinia? Is she . . . ?"

"She is very weak but we trust no lasting damage has been done. The doctor is with her now," Aurora assured him at once.

"Thank God." The baron mopped his perspiring brow with a fine handkerchief. "Pray be seated, Miss Marshingham, and tell me what brings you to my humble lodgings."

Not so very humble, concluded Aurora, observing the heavy red damask curtains and the thick rug on the floor. The furniture too was of the first stare and obviously quite expensive.

"May I offer you some refreshments?" offered the baron.

"No, thank you. This is no time for civilities."

Aurora perched on a corner of a settee. The baron remained standing. "I come with a message from Lady Lanville. She is beside herself at the thought of your meeting Lord Roxton, and she begs you not to go through with it. Inform Lord Roxton that you have changed your mind and won't meet him after all."

"Impossible. I cannot do it," the baron said.

"She is afraid you might be killed," Aurora explained.

"To be perfectly frank, Miss Marshingham, so am I. I do not desire this duel any more than she, but I cannot cry off."

"You shouldn't have accepted his challenge in the first place. It was most imprudent—if he is as good a shot as Lady Lanville says he is."

"He is," the baron said glumly. "And my accepting his challenge was the height of folly. I don't mind admitting it to you, Miss Marshingham. But—" He took a quick turn about the room. "I have stood countless insults and interference from Roxton, and I have always managed to swallow them. But today—today was the outside of enough. His behavior was such—His insults—It was more than the flesh could bear. So I accepted. And I cannot and will not cry off."

"But Lady Lanville is afraid that the earl will kill you. And y-you just admitted—" Aurora stammered.

"Let us hope that Roxton's rage has abated enough by the time we meet so that he won't shoot to kill. He might wish to kill me when in the heat of passion, but not when he has allowed his anger to cool and had time to reflect on the matter."

He gave her a rueful smile. "Alas, my accomplishments do not include being an excellent shot. The mere thought of the duel makes me shudder; but no, no, Miss Marshingham, I cannot cry off."

"I think you are very brave, Lord Style, to insist on going through with it," Aurora told him. "And I think Lord Roxton is very stupid, besides being quite hateful. I wish I had the power of prevailing upon him not to meet you after all. But I'm afraid my intercession would only make matters worse."

The baron rubbed the side of his nose in a speculative manner. "Oh, one never knows. I am persuaded he likes you a great deal."

"Lord Style, how can you be so absurd!" Aurora cried. "Have you forgotten how he abused me at the masquerade? And since! The names he has called me! Do you really ask me to beg him—"

"No, no, no. I do not ask you anything. Out of the question! I shall just have to meet him. There is nothing for it!"

Aurora rose from her seat. "Is that what I shall tell Lady Lanville?"

"Tell her I will take dashed good care not to get killed. And . . . give her my love." He sighed. "Poor Vinny. He is making her life so miserable. Just for that I wish I could wing him. Not kill, mind, just wing." He touched the bell pull.

Drawing on her gloves, Aurora was hurriedly walking down the steps of Lord Style's lodgings when a vehicle approached the house. Aghast, she saw Lord Roxton's curricle come to a halt. Lord Roxton was staring at her with a sardonic curl to his lip, his gray eyes hard as granite, the angle of his chin stiff and severe.

"So! I have my answer at last! You *are* his light-o'-love. The minute my back is turned, you run to him. Well"—he bared his teeth in an evil grimace—"you *shan't* be running to him much longer, my girl; for after tomorrow he shall be dead!"

Aurora stepped closer to the curricle. "Lord Roxton, you are greatly mistaken in Lord Style. I am not considering myself in the matter, pray believe me! It is Lady Lanville, your sister-in-law, I am thinking of most of all. She loves him and she shall be desolated——"

"She cannot love him much when she allows his Cyprian to stay in Berkeley Square," the earl snapped. "And for your information, my girl, I have been considering her illness and her fondness for Alphonsus. I was on my way to Style with the intention of telling him to forget all about that duel, but I have changed my mind."

"Oh, no!" Aurora cried in cold dismay while her hand flew to her mouth. "Oh, no!"

"Oh, *yes!* You should have done better not to rush to console him in such haste."

"But I didn't. Lady Lanville begged me to go."

"A likely story."

"It is true!" Aurora cried.

He shrugged. "It is of no consequence. Get up."

"What?"

"Get up into the curricle."

"I will *not!*" said Aurora, much outraged.

"You will, if I have to jump down and throw you in. And don't think I can't do it."

"I shall go in a hackney. I have money this time."

He gave a sharp laugh. "I am not being chivalrous. Don't give yourself false notions on that score. I don't want you running to him again. You shall return to Berkeley Square and stay there until after I have disposed of him, after the duel."

"You have taken leave of your senses, my lord," Aurora cried. "You cannot mean what you say."

"I mean every word."

"But——"

The earl leaned over quickly. One strong hand closed itself like a vise on Aurora's arm. The horses, sensing a disturbance, fidgeted and snorted. "Come on, you can climb up unassisted, I know."

Aurora gritted her teeth. "In all my life I have never encountered anyone with less manners than you. Very well. I'll go with you, but only because you constrain me to, and

I don't wish to create a scene. Just look at those people—gaping already!"

"Yokels and cits. What do you care about them? Up!" And his strong arm assisted her, almost pulled her into the curricle and onto the seat beside him.

Aurora sat stiffly erect, staring ahead with unseeing eyes as the vehicle proceeded through the streets of London at a smart pace.

The earl preserved a stony silence, not deigning to speak or look in her direction. Once or twice Aurora stole a glance at his profile. His expression was uncompromising and rigid, his lips compressed into a hard line. Every feature of his face registered strong disapproval and contempt.

Aurora's heart swelled with hurt and anger. How she loathed that man! From the first moment of meeting her he had set out to humiliate and insult her, yet he had the temerity to suggest that her fate was *his* concern. He *must* have taken leave of his senses. But had he really intended calling off the duel? And did her appearance on the scene change his mind? She would not forgive herself were it so. In spite of her hatred and rage, she was compelled to speak out once more.

"Lord Roxton," she began rather diffidently, then she tossed her head defiantly. "Lord Roxton," she repeated more strongly, "I do not know why my calling on Lord Style should have changed your mind about fighting him, but if indeed it was so, pray reconsider. What does my person matter when compared with the fate of Lady Lanville and the life of the baron? Why should your anger at me—incomprehensible to me as it is—destroy her life and that of the baron? I do not matter here at all."

A strange fire of bitterness and hate and—and something else leaped into the earl's eyes as he turned his head toward her. "Oh, but you *do* matter," he said in a harsh voice. "And, moreover, *you* know it. Do not deny it! You know it."

Aurora was astonished. "I . . . know it? Know what?"

"You must know. Surely those yokels in Yorkshire—" He broke off abruptly. "Oh, no! That is precisely what you want, you jade. Well, it won't work."

"My lord, your words are entirely incomprehensible to

me," Aurora cried, but her heart pounded uncomfortably withal.

"Oh, are they?" he sneered. "Don't pretend to be so innocent."

Aurora's blue eyes flashed with outrage. "Lord Roxton, I have had just about enough of your insults and your high-handed manners. And I do not wish to spend a single minute more in your company. Pray stop the carriage so I can alight."

The earl disregarded her request.

"I beg you to stop the carriage this instant," Aurora insisted. "I am persuaded that round the next corner is a hackney stand and—"

Her answer was the snap of the earl's whip as he spurred on the horses to a quicker pace. They responded with a thundering of hoofs, galloping down the street, sending urchins and dogs scampering for cover.

"Take care, my lord! We are coming to a corner." But the earl, savage and grim, paid no heed to her words.

"My lord, you will overturn the carriage!" Aurora almost screamed as the curricle swayed dangerously from side to side. Should she jump before that happened? But of course she could not attempt it. Instead, she tried to grapple with him for the reins, to halt the horses' wild run. "Slow down, slow down, my lord!" she cried, as she attempted to possess herself of the reins.

The earl gave her a strong shove that almost swept her off the curricle. She tried to recover her balance, but they were coming round the bend with great speed, and Aurora, arms flailing wildly, was thrown against the earl.

Instinctively his one arm went about her shoulders to prevent her from being thrown to the ground as the curricle now swayed perilously to the other side.

Aurora, panting heavily, her hood slipped back, her hair dishevelled, lay against his broad shoulder, hanging on to him for dear life. Then they were round the corner and the earl was slacking the pace, controlling the horses with one hand, while the other still held her to his side. They were coming to a halt.

Aurora dared to lift her head. "My lord, you are a shockingly reckless driver," she began but broke off as she stared into those usually impenetrable gray eyes, so close to her own. Now they were alight with a strange fire. His severe lips were slighted parted, revealing his strong white teeth. Aurora could feel his hot breath on her face.

And abruptly she was in his arms, crushed in a tight embrace that almost squeezed the breath out of her body, while his hungry lips fastened onto hers in a ruthless, bruising kiss.

Aurora froze in horror and shock. And yet while her mind was still paralyzed by the suddenness of his attack, her lips—for an infinitesimal span of time—found themselves responding to the force and desire of his lips. For one split second time was suspended as her heart answered his unspoken call.

But only for that moment. In the next she was pushing feebly at his chest, trying to free herself. "How dare you, my lord!" she gasped out. And the earl, as if recollecting himself and his surroundings, suddenly flung her away from him with a strong gesture of disgust. His countenance was a dull red, his lips once more compressed and severe. Firmly he grasped the reins and guided the nervous horses with a steady hand and in complete silence the rest of the way to Berkeley Square.

Aurora, her cheeks burning with anger at his scandalous behavior and shame at her own brief response to his kiss, stared straight ahead, not daring to cast another glance at him. At Berkeley Square he jumped down, and Aurora, not waiting to see whether he would help her alight, clambered down also and preceded him up the stairs.

She went at once to Lady Lanville's bedchamber. The earl followed her. But at the door to Lady Lanville's chamber, Bellman stood with arms crossed on her chest and refused to let him in.

"You cannot go in, your lordship. Doctor's orders," she said, her normally stern face even more severe with disapproval and reproach. "You have done enough damage for one day."

The earl scowled at her. "She is better, isn't she? The doctor said she will recover."

"She will, but only if she does not sustain any more agitation of the nerves. If I may venture to say, my lord, one look at your lordship's countenance now would throw her into strong hysterics."

The earl appeared nonplussed for a moment, then abruptly he turned on his heel and began to walk away. After a few steps he halted, just as Aurora was about to disappear into the bedchamber. "I expect you to stay in the house, Miss Marshingham. Do not disappoint me," he added in an icy tone that held in it a note of threat. Then he was gone.

Aurora stared after him in cold fury, then entered Lavinia's room.

Lavinia lifted herself on one elbow and pounced on Aurora eagerly. "Did you see Alphonsus? What did he say? Did he promise not to meet Roxton?"

Aurora regretfully shook her head. "I am afraid he is adamant. He cannot cry off now."

The widow gave a despairing moan. "But he will be killed! Roxton will kill him. You must beg Roxton not to meet him. You must."

"I did ask. I begged him to spare your feelings. He would not listen. But Lord Style assures you there is no need to worry. Lord Roxton will not shoot to kill."

"But he will!" wailed Lavinia, growing more agitated by the second. "You have failed me, and I was so certain you would help. Oh, Alphonsus, I shall lose you now for sure!"

"My lady, pray do not distress yourself," cried Bellman, fluttering about her mistress.

"But Lord Style assured me," interjected Aurora, "that once Lord Roxton's anger has cooled, he won't want to really harm him. Now, Lavinia, for God's sake, don't carry on so," Aurora exclaimed as Lavinia began to thrash about and emit hysterical cries. "I shall try again to prevent the meeting. I am persuaded I will find a way—only I must have a little time to think. Now calm yourself."

But the widow fell into hysterical sobbing, and Bellman motioned for Aurora to leave the room. "You shouldn't have told her that, miss. You should have made up a tale."

"But—"

"Pray leave me to deal with her. I know how. She feels

you have failed her, and your presence here will only upset her all the more."

"I'm sorry, Lavinia, to have distressed you. And I will try again to stop the duel."

"I hope I have not caused her to have a severe setback," she muttered as Bellman ushered her out of the room and locked the door behind her.

- 17 -

AURORA WAS TRULY sorry for the widow, but she was also a bit vexed. How could Lavinia blame her for not being able to persuade the baron or the earl to forget all about that silly duel? In a matter of "honor," Aurora thought with contempt, men behaved with a remarkable lack of common sense. Yet the baron would have found it hard to withdraw once he had accepted the challenge. As for the earl, if he really wanted to forget all about it, why should her appearance on the scene have incensed him so? Could it be? No, no. And yet . . . there was that demanding kiss. She could still feel it burning on her lips.

Once more blood mounted to her cheeks as she thought of those strong arms crushing her. She took a deep breath, trying to steady herself. The earl could not have meant anything by that kiss. He hated her and thought her beneath contempt. Then why was he moved to kiss her thus?

No. She would not think of it. She must not. Rather, she ought to think how to prevent the earl from killing Lord Style. But the more she thought of it, the more she became convinced that even if they did meet, the earl would not shoot to kill but merely to wound. Should she then try once more to interfere? Aurora was getting heartily sick of the whole matter and wished she was back home in Yorkshire. But she could not leave without knowing the outcome of the events.

The Viscount Deberough, who came later to inquire after Lavinia, reassured Aurora somewhat. He was full of talk about Melanie, but he was also of the opinion that the earl would not kill Lord Style. The viscount desired the duel no more than the widow, but he was not unduly concerned over the baron's life and even prophesized that the earl might withdraw his challenge. At all events, the time and the place of the meeting had not yet been set, for he would have known of it.

After the viscount had left, Aurora, worn out with the difficult events and conflicting emotions, decided that a short repose would do much to restore to her a clear head. But because she was certain she would not be able to fall asleep, she departed from her custom never to seek such help and took a few drops of laudanum, then climbed into bed.

She had intended to sleep only for an hour or so, but when she awoke, night had already fallen.

She yawned and rubbed her heavy eyes and rang for the maid. Nancy, the third parlormaid, answered her call. She lighted the sconces and pulled the curtains across the windows.

"How is Lady Lanville?" Aurora inquired, stretching in her bed.

The little maid shook her head sadly. "She is crying her eyes out, poor soul."

Aurora sat bolt upright. "Has something else untoward occurred?" she asked with apprehension. "The Baron of Style?"

"His lordship is well. That I do know, for Perkins was in to see her ladyship."

"Perkins?"

"His lordship's valet."

"You mean Baron Style's valet?"

The girl nodded.

That shifty-eyed individual. Aurora recalled the man, for he had opened the door of the Baron's lodgings.

"What would Lady Lanville be about with the likes of him?" she wondered aloud.

"I'm sure I couldn't say, ma'am. But"—the maid lowered her voice and glanced furtively around—"Bellman went out somewhere in the afternoon on an errand for milady, an' it weren't long after she came back that Perkins showed up. Said he had a message for her ladyship, which he would deliver only into her own hands. Bellman wouldn't let him in to see her ladyship, but her ladyship commanded to fetch him to her bedchamber and told Bellman to leave. Put her nose out of joint proper, it did," she added with satisfaction. Evidently Lavinia's personal maid wasn't much liked by other servants.

Then, as if recollecting that she had spoken too much, the girl added, "But, oh, pray miss, don't tell her I said that, for she would have me turned off, she would."

"Be easy on that score, I don't intend to," Aurora said as she was making herself presentable. "I will have some tea in my room. Leave it in the pot for I shall pour it myself."

But the maid was all agog with the unusual goings-on and continued in a confidential manner, "And then, after he had left, much after, Bellman and her ladyship had words. They was quite vexed with each other, only we couldn't hear—" She broke off, raising scared eyes to Aurora.

"You shouldn't listen at the keyholes," Aurora admonished her, "but I suppose today was an exceptional day. Only don't you and the others make a habit of it."

The girl let out a breath of relief. "Yes, miss. Well, Bellman was fit to be tied, and she rushed out of the house with her hat askew and was gone a long time. When she returned, her face was grim, and she marched right up to her ladyship and started upbraiding her for something and wished to know something about 'precisely what Lady Lanville had done.' Lady Lanville wouldn't tell her. That I do know, for I was asked to fetch some hot water for her ladyship, and I knocked on the door, only I daresay they didn't hear me, and I opened the door and I heard Bellman scolding Lady Lanville and—"

"I don't wish to hear any more," Aurora interrupted. "And don't gossip about it with the others. You may leave."

"Yes, ma'am." The girl curtsied and withdrew.

Aurora threw a light wrap around her shoulders and hurried to Lavinia's bedroom. What new fix had the widow got into now? she wondered with vexation. Even laid up in her bed, she couldn't help stirring up trouble.

Aurora knocked on the door from behind which could be heard the unmistakable sounds of sobbing. Without waiting to be bidden to enter, she walked in.

Lady Lanville was weeping into her pillow, and Bellman, the maid, towered above her with a disapproving look.

"Lavinia! Bellman, what new trouble has befallen her ladyship? Or is it merely an attack of the vapors?"

"Aye, it is an attack of the vapors to be sure, and it will be much worse if what I am suspicioning is true," the maid answered.

"In heaven's name, Lavinia, what's happened now?" cried Aurora.

The widow lifted her tearstained face. "Oh, Aurora," she moaned, "what shall I do? How can I undo it? Oh..."

Aurora turned questioning eyes on Bellman, who shrugged truculently. "Some harebrained dangerous scheme her ladyship has hatched up with Perkins. She didn't invite *me* into her confidence." Evidently that was the sore point with the maid.

Aurora approached the bed. "Lavinia, you must tell me at once what scrape you are in this time. I think that perhaps you ought to leave, Bellman. Perhaps I can worm it out of her ladyship, and then we may be able to prevent whatever it is."

Bellman looked mutinous but Aurora added, "If it is something to do with that infernal duel, as I collect it is, the sooner we get to the bottom of it, the better. Obviously Lady Lanville does not feel like confiding in you at present, and I don't think we have time to waste until she does."

Bellman hesitated, then heaved a deep sigh and nodded. "As you wish, Miss Marshingham. But pray do not hesitate to ask my assistance in anything to get her ladyship out of the scrape."

"Yes, yes, to be sure. Now go." After the maid had departed, Aurora said purposefully, "Now, Lavinia, tell me quickly what you have done and why you want to undo it."

"Oh," moaned the widow, "I do not wish James to be killed. I am not perfectly sure I wish him even wounded," she sobbed. "After all is said and done, he has been quite good to me. He is dreadfully strict and he hates Alphonsus, but—but—he is Will's brother, and I couldn't bear it if I was to be the cause of his death!"

Alarm shot through Aurora. "How could you, laid up in your bed, be the cause of Lord Roxton's death?" she asked. The widow continued to utter unintelligible phrases, and Aurora gave her shoulder a strong shake. "Lavinia, pull yourself together! What mischief have you planned for Lord Roxton?"

"Oh," the widow moaned and gave every indication of falling into a strong fit of hysterics.

Aurora did not hesitate long. She slapped her cousin smartly on the cheek.

Lady Lanville gasped, gulped, her eyes opened wide, her mouth likewise, but the shrieking and sobbing stopped as if by magic.

"Tell me at once!" Aurora commanded. "If I'm to undo what you have done, I must know all, at once." Her heart was pounding uncomfortably; her throat was dry. Concern for the earl was uppermost in her mind.

"It's too late," the widow cried. "Bellman couldn't find Perkins or Alphonsus—"

Aurora stamped her foot. "Lavinia, do you want *another* slap on the cheek?"

The widow tried to look outraged but merely succeeded in appearing pathetic. "I—I . . . asked Perkins, I opined that if only Roxton were in no condition to meet Alphonsus . . . I wanted him incapacitated." She gulped. "So I persuaded and I paid Perkins, though to be sure he would have done it even without money: he is very devoted to Alphonsus. I persuaded Perkins to waylay Roxton on his way home from the opera—it is his custom to walk, you see—and—and shoot him."

"What!" Aurora couldn't believe her ears.

"I didn't mean for Perkins to *kill* him. But, oh, what if perchance he should? Alphonsus once told me he is no mean

shot. And he might be thinking he would be doing his master
a favor by dispatching Roxton. Oh, I'm afraid he might kill
him. What shall I do?"

An intense cold settled in Aurora's heart. Lord Roxton
dead. That autocratic, hateful voice stilled forever. Those
hard, mocking gray eyes never to look on her again. *No!*
Something screamed within her. Something squeezed at her
throat, choked her. Tears welled up in her eyes. She couldn't
let that happen. She *couldn't.* No matter how he treated her,
she could not let him die.

"I must warn him," she cried. "I must seek him out
before he leaves the opera."

Lavinia propped herself on her elbows. "You are never
going to tell him the truth! He will put me in Bedlam—for
of course he wouldn't stand the scandal of having me arrested."

"Don't be an idiot. I won't tell him how I know, or who
had planned it."

The widow fell back on the pillows. "Oh, but it is too
late! He must be even now leaving the opera. It is quite
late."

Aurora tugged impatiently at the bell rope, and immediately Bellman materialized in the room.

"Desire a groom to fetch me the late Lord Lanville's
curricle. With the fastest horses." And as Bellman gaped
at her, Aurora exclaimed, "Don't waste time, if you don't
want Lord Roxton's death on your conscience and the worst
scandal of the century—" That did it. Bellman might not
have cared much for the earl, but the merest hint of a scandal
was enough to make her scuttle out of sight. "Pray that I'll
be in time," Aurora cried to Lavinia as she hurried out of
the room to her own chamber to throw a cloak over her
gown.

A short moment later she was running down the wide
staircase to the front door and impatiently waiting for the
curricle to be brought round. Fortunately she knew the direction of the opera house and thought she would know how
to get from there to Mount Street. In a few minutes she was
climbing into the curricle, over the protestations of the
groom, who wished to go along. But she couldn't have
witnesses to what she was about to impart to the earl. She

picked up the reins and the whip and set off at a smart pace. She hadn't driven such a sporting vehicle for some years, and this was a pair of spirited horses, but she had been quite a whip once, and she had no fear of not being able to control the pair.

The horses' hoofs thundered along the road as Aurora urged the animals on to an even faster gait, heedless of the traffic, taking the corners at too great a speed. All she could think of was how to reach Lord Roxton in time. Her throat was dry, her heart pounding. She did not stop to question her feelings; there was no time for it now. She had to concentrate on negotiating the streets and on not overturning the curricle, but she knew that, were she to arrive too late to prevent his death, something in her would die too.

The hood slipped off her head, revealing her hair gleaming in the lamplight. She paid no heed but drove on. At last she reined in before the opera house. But alas, the doors were closing and only a handful of patrons were leaving the edifice. Aurora hailed a groom waiting beside a carriage. "Pray, tell me, have you seen Lord Roxton leave?" she asked.

The man just stared at her, then shook his head.

Aurora, keeping the frisky horses under control with difficulty, repeated her question several times in vain, until a gentleman in an opera cloak and top hat, who was entering his carriage, heard her inquiry and imparted to her the knowledge that he had seen the earl leave right after the performance. Aurora thanked him and set out at once for Mount Street.

The streets were becoming more and more empty of people. The horses' hoofs and the curricle's wheels sent hollow echoes through the night. Here and there Aurora passed a vehicle, a group of late strollers, an occasional gentleman in evening cloak and hat. But no Lord Roxton.

At last, after what seemed to her impatient heart like hours, there, a few yards ahead of her she saw . . . *him*. She could not be mistaken in that tall, powerful frame and those broad shoulders. The whip crashed as she spurred on the horses. Should she call out to him now?

Her eyes searched the shadows in the streets. Was someone lurking there?

The horses were almost abreast of him.

The earl, not concerned by the thundering vehicle and hoofs, was sauntering along.

"Lord Roxton, take care!" Aurora shouted and pulled the horses to a sharp stop.

The earl whirled at the sound of her voice, and at that instant a shot rang out and reverberated in the stillness of the night.

The earl reeled and grabbed at his side, while Aurora made a leaping jump from the curricle and rushed toward the staggering man. Throwing herself at him, she felled him to the ground even as another shot rang out.

"Don't Perkins! Don't shoot!" she shouted.

There were no more shots. An eerie silence abruptly enveloped them, interrupted only by the champing of the horses. Then came the sudden clatter of feet. Aurora raised her head. A shadowy figure was running down the street.

Aurora felt limp with relief. But only for a moment. When she picked herself up from the ground and stared at the inanimate form of the earl, a large stain of blood spreading quickly on his chest, she felt a stab of pain in her heart. No! He could not be dead. He could not!

She fell on her knees beside him and cradled the still head in her lap. Tears poured freely down her cheeks. It was no use pretending to herself any longer. No matter what he was or how he treated her, she loved him. She loved him. And he was dead. And she—she was the indirect cause of his death. Grief and despair gripped her by the throat and threatened to overcome her senses.

A weak moan made her start.

Was it possible? Was he still alive? She groped for his hand, found the pulse. It was weak but, oh, thank God, it could still be felt. But he was bleeding profusely.

"Help, help," screamed Aurora, while she tore the cravat off his neck and tried ineffectively to staunch the bleeding.

Feet clattered on the pavement, voices cried out from the darkness. In the light of a lamp she saw a constable approaching at a run. And another. And other people, attracted by her shouts and the commotion.

"A surgeon. He's bleeding badly. Staunch the bleeding," Aurora gasped out.

One of the constables bent down. "Here, ma'am, let me do it. I know how. Hey, Clem, ge fetch the nearest doctor. And you, somebody, knock on the doors of one of these houses. We must get him inside."

"He l-l-lives in Mount Street. It is Lord Roxton," said Aurora. Her teeth were chattering from horror and shock.

"I know his house," said a man at Aurora's elbow.

"He's bleeding like a pig," another voice commented.

"Nasty wound," the constable agreed, while fashioning a pad out of a large handkerchief and pressing it against the wound. "That blimey cloak is in the way," he swore.

Aurora's senses reeled. She felt someone grab her by the shoulders, heard someone call, "Hey, she's going off into a swoon," and vaguely wondered who the man was talking about—before she stopped wondering at all.

- *18* -

AURORA REVIVED IN the bright light of a dozen sconces illuminating a salon of singular elegance and beauty. Bewildered, she blinked her eyes at the crystal chandeliers hanging from the high painted ceiling, at the gold-and-white decor of the drapes and the satin sofas, the deep pile rug on the floor. Where was she? What had happened? And then as she recalled, she sat up with a jerk, though her head was swimming. The earl!

"Is the earl dead?"

"No, ma'am. Leastways, not yet. The doctor is with him now."

Aurora turned in the direction of the voice. She hadn't realized she had posed her question aloud. The person who answered was a young maid with her cap askew and her apron spattered with blood.

Still alive. Oh, thank God! But would he live? Would he recover?

"Help me to my feet. I must go to him."

"On, no, no, my lady. You cannot help him now."

"I must. I—"

"Pray do not be worrying yourself," the girl said. "He is in good hands. Dr. Shiefer is a good doctor."

Aurora rubbed her brow. "How . . . ? Where am I?"

"In Mount Street. His lordship's lodgings."

"Ah! And you? Are you a servant here?"

"No, ma'am. I be with the doctor. When they came to fetch him, they said as they needed a female to attend to a lady. So I—I went."

"I'm much obliged to you." Aurora stared stupidly at her bloodstained gown. "Is he—is he badly hurt?" she asked, feeling faint with the fear for his Troy.

"I can't rightly say, ma'am. I heard them talking as the wound was clean but in a bad place—if you know what that means."

"I must go to him, I must!" She took a deep breath. "This won't do. How came I to swoon? I have never swooned in my life."

"Oh, it's not to be wondered at! Such a turn as it gave me to see his lordship all covered with blood. I near swooned myself!"

"Somebody must be dispatched to Brook Street, to the Viscount Deberough. He must know."

"Is that his lordship's brother?"

"Yes."

"Oh, he's been sent for already. He's abovestairs, with them."

Aurora rubbed her brow again, which was hurting very much for some reason. "How long was I out?"

"Quite some time. You hurt your head when you fell."

"It doesn't signify. Is the viscount—is Lord Roxton's brother with him in the bedchamber?"

"No. Leastways I collect the doctor told him to wait outside the door of the bedchamber."

"Desire him to come down. I wish to talk to him," Aurora requested.

"Yes, ma'am. Right away." The maid curtsied and withdrew.

A few moments later the Viscount Deberough entered the salon. His face was pale and registered shock. His usually elegant attire was somewhat disarrayed.

He approached her with outstretched hands. "I am glad you are more the thing," he said warmly.

"How—how is he? Will he live?"

"He has lost a good deal of blood, and the bullet went perilously close to the heart, but fortunately no vital organs have been damaged. Dr. Shiefer has every hope of his recovery."

"Thank God for that."

"He has just finished tending to his wound and will come directly to take a look at you."

"Oh, *I* don't signify. I want to stay here and nurse him," Aurora announced.

The viscount eyed her dubiously. "I'm not at all sure that is wise. You're quite knocked up yourself, and you need a change of clothes. But pray tell me how came he to be shot. I collect he was walking home from the opera, as was his custom. Was he set upon? And how came you to be in the neighborhood at this time of night? You must be a first-rate whip if you contrived to drive Will's grays and his sporting curricle. I own I couldn't believe it to be true. But one of the local constables recognized Will's horses."

"I—I . . ." Aurora forced her benumbed brain to a glib explanation. "Lady Lanville was so upset. I wished to seek out his lordship and beg him once more not to meet with Lord Style. I came upon him just as . . . just as . . ." She swallowed hard and could not go on.

"Don't! Do not distress yourself. You will tell me all about it anon," Albert said kindly. "Now you must rest until the doctor has seen to you, and then I shall drive you back to Berkeley Square."

Aurora started to protest, but found her head swimming again and was forced to lie down and close her eyes. Then the doctor came, and he and Lord Albert both tried to persuade her to give up her notion of staying in Mount Street to nurse the earl. The doctor assured her that the earl's valet would make a capital nurse, and Lord Albert informed her that he would keep watch beside his brother, so there was no need to put herself out. The doctor also opined, after attending to her hurts, that she needed a change of clothes, and one glance in the mirror showed her the reason for this notion. She looked a veritable fright, with her disheveled hair and muddied garments.

Reluctantly, she let herself be persuaded, allowing Lord Albert to drive her back to Berkeley Square, but not until the doctor had gone and the earl had fallen into an uneasy slumber. And also not until she had told her tale to the constables (without divulging to them the reason for her seeking out his lordship at this time of the night) and informed them that she had not been able to see the fleeing assailant, therefore could not identify him. If they disbelieved her, they kept that fact to themselves. Lord Albert promised to inform her in the morning how the earl was going on, and returned to Mount Street.

Aurora had had full intentions of returning there herself, but by the time she had bathed and changed into her nightgown, Lady Lanville had claimed her full attention. She was suffering in the worst possible way from the vapors, and this time at least she had a good reason to. She had heard of the earl's being shot and surmised the worst. It took the combined efforts of Bellman and Aurora to convince her that the earl would not succumb to his wound, that no one knew who had fired the shot, and that no one would blame the baron.

By the time Lady Lanville, plied with hartshorn and laudanum, had fallen asleep at last, Aurora was scarcely able to keep on her feet. She sought her bedchamber. In spite of her turbulent emotions and her fear and worry for the earl, she fell quickly into a deep sleep and wakened only when the maid was pulling open the curtains with the start of another day.

Aurora hated to stir, hated to leave the luxury of slumber. But as full memory returned, she sat upright, rubbing her eyes.

"How is Lord Roxton?" she inquired with trepidation.

"He is in a fever, but that is to be expected. Nothing to worry about, his lordship said."

"Which lordship?"

"The viscount. He was here and left word for you, ma'am, not to worry. And to tell you he stayed up with Lord Roxton all night and that the doctor has been in to see him again."

Aurora sighed with relief. "Pray what time is it?"

"It is after ten, miss. I didn't wish to wake you sooner."

"You should have. I have overslept again. How is Lady Lanville?"

The maid grimaced. "As well as can be expected. Baron Style is with her now. And a rare trimming he has given her too, from what Bellman let fall."

"I'm sure Bellman knows better than to gossip about her mistress," Aurora said sharply, and the girl grew silent under the rebuke and presently withdrew.

While Aurora washed and dressed, she took a quick stock of her feelings and her present state of affairs. It was a melancholy reflection to know herself to be in love with a man who only despised her. To know that she could never hope for his love in return. And the way he treated her, she ought not to desire love, ought to feel only hate and contempt for him. But—She shook her head impatiently. She was not a moonstruck schoolgirl. She was three and twenty and ought to know better. Having been hurt once, she ought not to have allowed herself to fall in love again, and especially not with the earl! She had her younger sisters to take care of; she could not afford indulging in hopeless passions.

For the first time Aurora did not feel out of patience with Priscilla. If she were indeed in love with her soldier . . . If only he could afford to buy himself a commission, perhaps she ought to let him marry Priscilla. At least *he* wished to marry her.

Aurora gave another impatient sigh. She ought to insist on Lavinia's finding her an eligible situation. Now perhaps the widow would listen more readily, now that she felt herself so much obliged to Aurora. For it seemed certain that if Aurora hadn't intervened, Perkins would have killed Lord Roxton. Whatever his reason for firing twice— whether he wasn't perfectly sure he had wounded the earl on the first try or whether, at the last moment and in a fit of rage, he had decided to rid his master of the constant vexation and obstacle to him that Lord Roxton repre- sented—he went beyond Lady Lanville's orders in almost putting a period to the earl's existence. Aurora wondered whether the widow had confided the whole to the baron. Probably she had, hence the gossip about a quarrel between them.

After partaking of a light breakfast, Aurora went to her

cousin's chamber, knocked lightly on the door, and entered. Lavinia, puff eyed but dressed in a fetching negligee and cap, rested in the baron's arms.

"I beg your pardon. I shall come back later," Aurora said.

"No need to go," said the baron, not at all discomfited or about to relinquish the widow. "Lavinia loves me," he said simply. The widow cast a worshipful look at his florid countenance. "How are you feeling, Miss Marshingham? I trust you have recovered from last night."

"Yes, thank you, Lord Style."

"We owe you a great debt of gratitude, Miss Marshingham."

Lavinia lifted her tearstained face from his shoulder. "Yes. Alphonsus said everything would have been ruined if you hadn't—hadn't—"

"I was glad I contrived to prevent a tragedy, if indeed I did so," Aurora said. "I came to see how you were, Lavinia, and if you needed any errands done. I shall have to go out and—"

"Will you—will you go by way of Mount Street?"

Aurora hesitated. That was indeed what she had in mind, but she was not sure whether it was the thing to do.

"For I would like to know how—how he is," Lavinia said. "And though Albert assures me he will not sustain a lasting harm, I could never forgive myself if—" She sniffled into a shredded handkerchief.

"Here, take mine," said the baron, thrusting one of his large, scented ones into her hands. "I ought to beat you, Vinny," he said severely.

"But I did it only because I couldn't bear the thought of losing you!" wailed the widow.

"That is the only reason I am not cutting you now," he said, but his glance was tender. "If you are going to Mount Street, Miss Marshingham, pray allow me to accompany you. I have to see James."

"Oh, dear. Ought you—"

"I must ascertain if he knows it was Perkins. Dash it, I've got to know! And he won't tell you or Albert. I've got to know what I'm in for," the baron said worriedly.

"Oh, I—I'm so sorry," Lavinia sniffled.

"Perhaps I can compel him to listen to me," the baron continued, "when he is not able to fly out at me or stalk off. Perhaps I can make him see reason not to stay in the way of our marriage; though I think I would be a fool to marry you, Vinny, after this escapade."

"Oh, Alphonsus!" the widow cried soulfully.

The baron gently disengaged her clinging hands. "You will permit it, Miss Marshingham?"

"If you insist. But pray be careful," Aurora begged. "I am persuaded he must be still quite feverish. It wouldn't do to make him worse."

"No fear of that—with you by my side to make sure I won't." The baron smiled, then turned to Lady Lanville. "Rest now, Vinny, and mind Bellman. And, oh, I have just thought of something. The children." He shook his head. "I'm afraid he would never allow me to become their step-papa." He shrugged. "Well, I can only try."

"Oh, Alphonsus! When you get on so famously with them!"

Aurora's eyes widened at this information.

"That's true," said the baron. "Vinny don't like to have them underfoot, but I have taken them and Vinny on a picnic once or twice. They were quite happy to crawl all over me. Ruined my cravat and my best waistcoat too." He grimaced at the reminiscence.

"And you let them," said Lavinia, her eyes alight with warmth.

"Well, I dashed well would make sure it would *not* become a habit with them, were I to become their papa. I can't have my clothes ruined by grubby fingers every day." But the baron was smiling broadly.

Aurora was astonished. Here was another side of Alphonsus she had not hitherto suspected.

"Mind, if they were not Vinny's children, I wouldn't have allowed it at all," the baron said as he rose, carefully straightened his coat and cravat, and removed an invisible speck of dirt from the sleeve of his coat.

Aurora was dubious of the advisability of her calling on the earl, especially with Lord Style. Thus it was with deep misgivings that she allowed the baron to drive her to the earl's lodgings. She would not have been surprised had the

baron been refused admittance. But the stolid butler who
opened the doors and ushered them in presented a polite
front and, upon Aurora's anxious question, assured them
that his lordship was much improved. As to whether he was
fit enough to receive visitors, he would go up and inquire.

But that did not suit the baron. "Never mind going up
to announce us. We shall announce ourselves," he said,
handing the butler his hat and gloves.

"Oh, but—he may be resting," objected Aurora. "Or—
or—"

"Exactly so, ma'am," said the butler. "I shall inquire.
If you be pleased to step this way." He was guiding them
to a salon.

"Well, I mean to see him whether he likes it or not,"
stated Lord Style. "This may be my only chance of getting
him to listen to me. What's more, you can't throw me out!"

The butler drew himself up. "I wouldn't try."

"Oh? You would send one of your flunkies to do the job,
would you?" the baron threw at him.

The butler ignored this remark and stalked off, very much
on his dignity.

"Pompous ass," the baron said with contempt. "Begging
your pardon. He's even more high in the instep than James.
Wouldn't have a fellow like that working for me for the
world." He paced the room back and forth.

Aurora, her heart pounding, her cheeks flushed, and her
thoughts on the earl, noticed only vaguely that the salon
was the same elegant chamber decorated in white and gold
to which she had been brought last night.

In moments the butler returned. "His lordship will see
you now," he announced in a wooden tone. There was just
a hint of surprise in his impassive countenance.

"Both of us?" asked Aurora quickly.

The butler hesitated. "I'm not perfectly sure . . . about the
lady."

But the baron would have none of it. "We shall go together, ma'am. You shall lend me moral support and make
sure that I don't overtax his lordship's strength." He hesitated, then added in a low tone, "He might not like talking
in front of witnesses, in which case you would be so obliging
as to leave the room for a short space."

"Certainly, Lord Style. Oh, I *do* hope he hasn't sustained a lasting injury."

"The doctor said he hasn't, didn't he? James has the constitution of an ox. Never fear he won't recover." He studied Aurora's features for a moment. "Like *that*, eh? Well, I wish you luck. And you have a job cut out for you."

The color in Aurora's cheeks heightened. "Whatever do you mean, Lord Style?" she asked stiffly. Did she betray herself so easily then? That would never do.

"Now, now, don't get on your high ropes with me, Miss Marshingham. I won't say another word," soothed the baron.

They followed the butler up the wide staircase to the upper floor and along a corridor lined with red carpet to a double door, on which the butler knocked lightly. It was opened immediately by a valet, who eyed the visitors with disfavor. "His lordship is not to be disturbed. The doctor gave express orders that he must be kept quiet."

A weak but familiar voice came from inside the chamber. "Let him in and remove yourself. And don't come in until I ring for you."

- 19 -

AURORA'S HEART THREATENED to jump out of her chest, it pounded so hard, and even the baron seemed a trifle discomposed, now that they were about to see the earl.

The valet stared dubiously at Aurora. "I'm not perfectly sure—" He shrugged and opened the door wider to let them in.

"You!" A cry escaped the earl's pale lips.

He was resting propped up on the pillows, looking very wan and drawn, a waxen pallor to his cheeks. Now a frown creased his brow.

Aurora greeted him in a shaky voice while the baron nodded carelessly. "I understood the butler to say that we may come up." She strove hard to keep her voice steady. "Didn't he inform you, my lord, that I had come to pay a call on you also?"

The earl moved his head restlessly from side to side. One of his arms was in a sling, but the other now gripped the coverlet and began to knead it. "No. That is, I never gave him the chance. As soon as he mentioned Style, I told him to fetch him. I—"

"Oh, what's that to the purpose," the baron said, approaching the bed. "You look mighty queer, James. Never saw you looking so pasty-faced in my life."

"Thanks to *you!*" the earl said bitterly. "But I disappointed you. I am still alive."

"If you think I had anything to do with that hole you got in your chest, you're quite mistaken. What's more, I don't want to see you dead, not really. Not that I haven't wished so many a time, but to think that I sent a footpad to shoot you full of holes— Demme, that's the outside of enough!"

The earl's brows drew together. "Do you mean to tell me you didn't instruct that rascally valet of yours to dispatch me with a bullet?"

"Of course, I didn't. Whatever gave you the idea it was Perkins who shot you?"

"Oh, come now, Style. I heard Miss Marshingham call out his name. You can't deny that, ma'am," he said, his gray eyes glinting at Aurora.

The baron glanced at her reproachfully.

"I—I—tried to save his life," Aurora defended herself.

The baron took a deep breath and released it. "Very well, so it was Perkins who shot you. But I assure you positively that I had nothing to do with it. I was not even aware of it. If I was, I would have put a stop to it at once. Good God, James, I—to shoot you or maybe even kill you, with all the world knowing of the bad feelings between us!"

"Apparently you were so eager to avoid fighting that duel you forgot to think of appearances." The earl was almost too weak to sneer.

"My lord, pray do not excite yourself," Aurora begged. "But it *is* true. Lord Style did not order his valet to shoot you."

"Did you?" the earl asked her.

"I? I?" Words failed Aurora at this effrontery.

"Enough, James," the baron interposed. "You owe Miss Marshingham your life. I was told how she felled you to the ground before another bullet could strike you. She shielded you with her body and screamed for help, before she herself swooned."

The earl's eyes now burned with a strange fire. "Is that true, Miss Marshingham?"

Aurora, flushed and trembling, nodded. "I did try to prevent your being killed, my lord."

"Why?"

"Why? Now, James, haven't you eyes in your head?" Alphonsus smiled.

"Lord Style, I beg you," Aurora said sharply.

"Come closer," the earl commanded Aurora.

With a wildly beating heart, Aurora drew near. The pallor of his face now gave way to an unhealthy flush.

"I'm afraid you are getting overexcited, my lord," she said. "Your pulse must be tumultuous."

"Damn my pulse! How came you to be on hand to rescue me? Did you know an attempt would be made on my life?" he demanded.

Aurora nodded. "Only I learned of it almost too late." She shuddered.

"Who ordered Perkins to shoot me?" the earl asked.

Aurora was silent.

"Answer me, ma'am."

"It is not for me to say, my lord. Actually, the first inkling I had of it was from something one of the servants said."

"But who—"

"Oh, leave her alone. You know she won't tell you," interjected the baron.

"Then you will. If you didn't send Perkins after me, who did? Who was so desirous of removing me from this earth?"

"No, no! You are all wrong about it!" cried Lord Style.

"Then pray enlighten me."

But the baron said nothing.

"My lord, I beg you, do not become so agitated," pleaded Aurora. "It will do you no good."

"I want to know who—"

Abruptly he broke off. And stared ahead stupefied. *"Of course.* How thickheaded of me! But that *she* could actually conspire to kill me..."

"No, no. You are wrong, dead wrong, Roxton."

"So—" The earl let out a long sigh. "It *was* Lavinia." He closed his eyes as if overcome by that knowledge. His countenance turned even paler.

"Oh, now look what we have done," exclaimed Aurora. "He has swooned. We had better call his valet and order him to fetch the doctor."

"No need," the earl said in a weak voice. "I haven't swooned." His eyes fluttered open. "That she actually could do *that!* And don't bother denying it, Alphonsus. She wishes me dead and she—"

"No, no, no. She never wanted you dead. She wanted to save *me!* She was convinced you would kill me in that damned duel. Well, I—I own I was a trifle anxious too, but I did credit you with enough sense to drop the silly business, once your temper had cooled, or at least just shoot to wing me."

"I was going to forget all about it too," the earl said with a quick glance at Aurora. The color mounted again to his cheeks.

Aurora said nothing, but her own cheeks were burning with mortification.

"You were!" exclaimed the baron. "Then why the deuce didn't you tell Lavinia? She was beside herself with fear of losing me. She loves me still, you see. But she never wished to see you dead. Never! Miss Marshingham can testify to that."

Aurora nodded. "Yes. It is true. She was overwhelmed with remorse and grief. Oh, dear, I ought not to have admitted it, for she is sure you will clap her in Bedlam once you know the whole."

"Nonsense. Roxton wouldn't do that. Would you, James? She isn't dicked in the nob, just bird-witted, and—and desperate."

"She must have a very poor notion of me, if she really thinks I could kill you, Alphonsus."

The baron stiffened. "Well, you never gave her cause to change her opinion of you."

"Never gave cause!" exploded the earl. "When I took care of her and the children, removed every burden from her shoulders, gave her a handsome allowance. And *she*— vapors and extravagancies and complaints. That's all the thanks I ever got from her!"

"I know." The baron smiled. "And I realize you tried to do well by her and did. But you don't understand Lavinia.

You don't know how to handle her. She wouldn't play *me* any of her tricks, and I would soon teach her how to curb her extravagance. But she is still young, James, and she yearns for parties and dances and such. Will was a good husband and he loved her, I'm sure, but he was much too staid. No, no"—he waved his well-cared-for hand—"I know what you are going to say. That Will was wild, that I made him—Well, maybe Will wished to lead a trifle less— less respectable life. But he couldn't really. He was a Lanville. What I'm trying to point out to you is that even with Will alive, life for Lavinia was rather dull. And now that she is a dowager and expected to behave with sedateness and decorum—Well, that sort of life drives her wild."

The earl stared at him, a strange expression on his face, not untinged with admiration. "I believe you *still* love her, after all these years! You still do. And I was quite sure you were keeping up the relationship just to spite me."

The baron gave an embarrassed cough. "To own the truth, I wasn't perfectly sure of my feelings myself, until I beheld her unconscious on the ground. Then I knew."

"So you love her and you know how to handle her. I actually believe you would make her a good husband," the earl said.

"Dash it, James, that's what I've been trying to convince you of. That she would be much better off married to me than spending her life as a disgruntled dowager."

"And you would be much better off to have your estates once more in the family." The earl sneered. "Don't try to bamboozle me with your noble motives."

"Dash it, Roxton, you just admitted I would be good for her. And I know how to handle the children too."

"No. I cannot allow it. Will was my brother. I cannot allow you—"

"He was my friend," Alphonsus interjected.

"And you drove him to his grave," retorted the earl.

"I did not. I was as much grieved at his passing as you."

The earl gave a sharp laugh. "How dare you! How dare you say that, after you plied him with drink and then forced him to make that crazy wager. You knew damn well he was in no state to handle a curricle and four spirited horses. He was three parts drunk."

"So was I. And I didn't force him." The baron passed his hand distractedly across his face. "Oh, God, don't you think, James, that I haven't blamed myself for that? That I haven't felt damned guilty for unwittingly contributing to his death? I swear to you, James, I never meant him to come to any harm. But I knew it would have been useless to try persuading you, any of you, of that. Even Albert. Only Lavinia knew I wouldn't have—at least she would have known, if you had told her of your dreadful suspicions that I deliberately egged him on to that bet. I didn't want Will dead." Beads of perspiration started on the baron's brow while the earl's visage paled even more alarmingly.

"Lord Style, I don't think—" Aurora started, but they were past remembering her presence. The earl's lips were tightly pressed.

After taking another deep breath, the baron continued. "We were drinking that night, quite heavily. And for good reason. Will was—Well, I think Will was just waking up to the fact that he had made a mistake when he married Lavinia, and as I heartily concurred in that...Well, we both played and talked and drank far too much. I don't recall how we came to talk of curricle racing. I used to be quite a good whip myself once, and we got to quarreling as to who was the better. I tell you we were both drunk. I can't recollect how that foolish wager came about. I think I remember telling Will that it wasn't a night for curricle racing—the weather—but he just laughed at me."

"Next you shall be telling me that you had actually endeavored to stop him," spat the earl.

"No. I disremember whether I did or did not. I told you I was foxed. I went to sleep soon after, and when I woke up, with as devilish a head as I ever had in my life, it was all over. The accident. And you and all the Lanvilles were breathing fire at me," the baron concluded.

"Then you didn't try to kill him deliberately?"

"For God's sake, James, what kind of a monster do you make me out to be? You've known me all your life!" Alphonsus declared.

"Yes, I have," said the earl with a sardonic curl to his lip. "And never have I known you to be any different—

gaming, drinking, the petticoats. You were a wild one, right enough."

"And you were the saintly Lanville. No wonder Will couldn't stomach you. He had more of the Wendover in him than all the rest of you put together," the baron went on. "He was a good chap, but between Lavinia's megrims and your insistence on propriety, you well nigh drove the poor fellow out of his wits."

"So!" A hissing sound escaped the earl's throat. "You think *I* am to blame! That *I* drove him to drink and thence to his death. And to be sure, I know I am to blame," he added bitterly. "I should have prevented his marrying Lavinia. I should have taken better care of him."

"Good God, James. You can't be serious! You couldn't have prevented that marriage if you'd tried. Old Lady Merton had set her heart on Lavinia's marrying Will. Nothing could have stopped *her*."

"I could have," the earl said stoutly.

"No, you couldn't. Not with Will and Lavinia fancying themselves in love with each other, and not with old Merton threatening that if Lavinia didn't marry Will, he'd give his consent to old Wentworth's suit. You remember him, sixty if he was a day, plagued with gout and the worst lecher in town. But he had a title. And money. Faced with that fate, what could Will have done but to marry her—in spite of all your opposition?"

The earl sank back against the pillows. "So that was it! And I never knew."

"Good God, I thought you did." The baron was surprised. "I thought everybody did. Though, to be sure, I didn't ascertain if you did or not, for as soon as I learned of Lavinia's engagement, I left town."

For the first time the earl's hard eyes softened. "Will was your friend, and he stole the girl you loved. And yet—and yet—" His expression hardened again. "Yet you mean to say that you didn't hate him, that you didn't want to take revenge on him?"

"Well, naturally, I wished him to the devil many times but revenge, no. No use blaming Will," the baron said reasonably. "He could have fancied himself in love with

Lavinia, but without Lavinia's—and the Mertons'—wanting it, he never would have married her. Lavinia wanted him, you see. The poor girl was dazzled by his good looks and fortune. She likes high living, as you well know. And what could *I* offer her?"

"You could have mended your ways, stopped your gaming, and stopped being so extravagant yourself."

"But my dear fellow, one has to live in style. Besides, well, in those days . . ." He shrugged. "The Mertons would never have countenanced our marriage. But I understood Lavinia. Maybe precisely because I am like her in many ways."

"And in spite of all that, in spite of the hurt she had inflicted upon you—" The earl shook his head. "Al—I—" He took a deep breath, his face beaded with perspiration. "It seems I have wronged you in thinking you deliberately lured Will to his death. I—" He stretched out his hand to the baron, and the baron grasped it in a firm grip.

"I think . . . you had better . . . better marry her after all. And get her out of my hair. But the children—I . . ."

"Lord Style, this is too much," cried Aurora, who had been loathe to interrupt this exchange of words, seeing that much misunderstanding was being cleared up, but now deciding she must. "He is going to swoon. He has swooned already!" She tugged hard on the bell rope, while the baron released the earl's limp hand and bent over him.

"Yes, I believe he has swooned this time."

The valet burst into the room. "His lordship?"

"Fetch the doctor. Get me some smelling salts," demanded Aurora. "Oh, my lord, my lord." She sobbed, beside herself with fear, kneeling on the floor by the bed and clasping his hand in hers. Had his health suffered a severe setback? But to her great relief, the doctor, when he presently arrived, was able to reassure her and Lord Style that the earl would weather this temporary reversal, provided he was left strictly alone, with no visitors allowed to call on him without the doctor's permission.

Lord Deberough came on the heels of the doctor to inquire after his brother and was very much astonished to find Lord Style making himself at home at Roxton House. He was even more astonished to hear that the earl had given his sanction to the baron's marriage with Lady Lanville. While the two men exchanged words, thrashing out old grievances and clearing up old misunderstandings, Aurora went to the guest chamber to straighten her attire and compose herself. Later, when Lord Deberough drove her to Berkeley Square, he appeared to be in rare good spirits. "Now there is no longer any reason for James's objecting to my paying court to Melanie. Was there anything more fortunate than this turn of events!" he exclaimed to Aurora.

"Well, really, my lord," Aurora objected. "How can you be so unfeeling! Here Lord Roxton is in high fever and all you can think of, all you can say is that nothing could be more fortunate!"

The viscount looked a trifle sheepish. "I don't mean I like James's being shot, but he will be up and about soon. And if it weren't for that, Style would never have dared to call on him and yet bring up that dreadful night of Will's accident. I'm glad Alphonsus isn't the blackguard we all thought him to be. Now Lavinia can have her wish, and Alphonsus too. For his lands will once more belong to the family. And I can marry Melanie. So his being shot was a piece of good luck. It's a small price to pay for having all the family problems settled in one swoop."

He was partly right too, Aurora conceded. If only she could rid herself of the worry about Lord Roxton's health.

She needn't have been concerned. After three nights of high fever, the earl's condition began to improve rapidly. His wound was mending well, and he was even allowed up for a few hours each day. All this Aurora learned from Lord Albert, who called in Berkeley Square every day, full of plans for himself and Melanie, who had been reestablished there. Lord Style also called freely now, and he and Lavinia spent long, happy hours discussing their forthcoming nuptials. Lady Lanville had been very moved upon hearing that the earl did not intend to punish her for her horrid deed and declared him a very good fellow after all.

With everybody in such high spirits, Aurora alone was beset by blue devils. The outcome may have been most fortunate for the others, but it had changed absolutely nothing for her. The earl might feel grateful to her for trying to save his life. In fact, he wrote her a very handsome letter and informed her that he would call on her as soon as he was up and about. But Aurora did not want his gratitude. And when she thought back on his outrageous proposal of marriage and realized he might repeat his offer, out of guilt combined with gratitude, she could have screamed with vexation!

She longed to be married to his lordship. But not when he thought her a scheming, cunning jade. And even were he to think well of her, she wanted his love, not his pity or gratitude. Yet she knew, were he to appear before her in all his handsomeness and splendor, that she would have a very hard time refusing his offer. In fact, she could not be perfectly sure she would be able to say no. And on no account must she say yes. She loved him, yes, loved him with her whole being, but she could not forget his odious behavior toward her, or the names he had called her. She had her pride. The only way out for her was to return to Yorkshire at once and stay there until Lavinia had secured an eligible post for her.

The thought did not fill Aurora's heart with joy, but she had never shirked from an unpleasant duty and would not do so now. Accordingly, she informed Lavinia that she was obliged to return to Yorkshire to take Priscilla, her sister, in hand, before that lovesick damsel eloped with her soldier beau. The widow demurred and deplored Aurora's departure, but she was so full of wedding plans, she had not much thought to spare for Aurora beyond saying that it was a *great* pity Aurora had to leave just then, for she could be of *so much* use to her now in her preparations for the wedding; and especially so since the cook, Mrs. Payne, who had turned out to be the one who carried tales to the earl, was prostrated with the vapors upon Lavinia's discovering her perfidy. Typical Lavinia, thought Aurora.

And so, with a heavy heart, Aurora departed for Yorkshire a day before the earl was to call on her in Berkeley Square.

- 20 -

TWO DAYS LATER, Aurora, in a yellow muslin frock, her auburn curls bound with a yellow ribbon, was seated by the window in her chamber at Hart Manor, her uncle's Yorkshire residence, trying to devise a plan that would enable her to cease being a burden on Aunt Martha and Uncle Horace and at the same time provide for her own and her sisters' future. But again and again before her mind's eye appeared a harsh, handsome countenance. A hard, cold voice rang in her ears, and her heart responded in spite of her resolve to forget all about *him*.

Through the half-open window the scent of flowers wafted to her nostrils. The buzzing of a bee accentuated the idyllic silence of the countryside. The house was silent too, for the servants—the few that still remained with them—were working on the estate, and Uncle Horace and Aunt Martha had gone with Adelina to a wedding. Only Aurora and Priscilla had chosen to remain at the manor, neither of them being in the mood for merriment and dancing.

Abruptly the quiet countryside was broken by the sound of horses' hoofs. Startled, Aurora lifted her head to survey the carriage drive and the road beyond.

The next moment a well-known curricle-and-four swept

around the bend. Aurora's heart leaped to her throat. No! It couldn't be! But it was. The Earl of Roxton—without his valet or even a groom—was driving in. Oh, the folly of it, to be driving himself in his enfeebled condition.

The earl pulled up his horses and jumped down from the curricle. Aurora gave a light exclamation and half rose in her chair as he swayed for a moment and had to hold on to the carriage. But the next instant he was at his horses' heads, steadying them, and then he was walking up the steps to the front door.

Aurora's heart was pounding, her chest heaving, but she remained seated as if paralyzed, unable to move.

The knocker sounded repeatedly before she heard Priscilla open the door. And then his voice. "My name is Roxton and I've come to call on Miss Marshingham, Miss Aurora Marshingham. Is she at home?"

"You—you are Lord Roxton," she heard Priscilla stammer in her hesitant voice. "But—but—we thought you were still laid up in your bed."

"Well, I'm not," the earl said crossly. "May I come in?"

"You may. Pray do so; but it won't do you any good. She won't see you," Priscilla added with an attempt at resolution. Aurora could almost see her swallowing convulsively.

The earl stepped over the threshold and the door swung shut.

A few moments later a soft knock sounded on the door of Aurora's bedchamber, and Priscilla entered. Her comely face and large eyes expressed both apprehension and wonder, while one of her hands unconsciously kneaded a fold of her sprigged muslin gown.

"Aurora, it is *he,* Lord Roxton! He begs to see you, to have a word with you. He is so elegant. And his greatcoat—so many capes. And, oh, Aurora." Priscilla pressed a hand to her palpitating bosom. "He said he would buy Bert a commission, if his own suit finds favor with you."

"What!" Aurora almost jumped out of her chair. "How dare he?"

"But Aurora, I think it is excessively handsome of him to offer, even though—" The corners of her lips twisted downward. "I know you will not have him. But—but—He

wishes to beg your pardon. Will you have a word with
him?"

"No. I thought I had made it plain to you that—"

"But I did tell him. I did inform his lordship that you
have no desire to see him. But he was adamant."

Aurora allowed herself a brief smile. He would be.

"I invited him into the parlor and helped him with his
greatcoat; but he said I shouldn't be doing it. And—Oh,
Aurora, the house is in such a shabby state, even though
we do try to keep it clean and tidy. The carpets are thread-
bare. What must he think? But there is no room better than
the front parlor—"

Aurora checked the girl's excited babble. "Do not be in
a taking over that. Just go and tell his lordship I do not wish
to see him." Her voice was even, but her pounding heart
and flushed countenance betrayed her conflicting emotions.

Half disappointed, half approving, Priscilla turned toward the door.

"Wait!" Aurora cried. "How is his lordship? His wound?"

"He seems a trifle weak and he asked for brandy."

"Then fetch it for him and let him rest in the parlor, but
on no account will I see him. Is that understood?"

Priscilla fled.

Aurora slowly rose from her chair, crossed the room,
and emerged in the corridor, her hands pressed to her heaving bosom, her ears straining for the sounds from below.
She could not, however, hear what was being said in the
parlor and was furious with herself for wishing to do so.

Abruptly she caught the sound of a door being opened
and the clatter of feet. Then Priscilla's voice was calling
urgently, "Aurora, Aurora, hurry pray! He is about to
swoon. Hurry! Help!"

Aurora, forgetting her resolution and her pride, rushed
headlong down the stairs and burst into the parlor.

The earl, his face pale and tense, rose to his feet, endeavoring to bow, but his legs buckled under him, and he
fell to his knees just as Aurora reached his side. The terrified
Priscilla stood wringing her hands helplessly.

"Oh, my lord!" exclaimed Aurora, placing her strong
arms around his shoulders.

Still on his knees, the earl lifted his head as a quizzical

smile played upon his lips. He managed to possess himself of her hand. Before he could speak up or do anything, however, Aurora said in a worried tone, "Let me assist you to the sofa, my lord. Priscilla, where is that brandy? Fetch it, then run over to Dr. Snyder and desire him to come immediately."

"A pox on all doctors," the earl said weakly. "But you are right on one account. Go, Miss Priscilla, go. I desire to beg Miss Marshingham's pardon in private."

"The brandy, Priscilla!" cried Aurora, stamping her foot. "Don't stand there gawking."

Priscilla revived from her stupefaction and scurried away.

"My lord—"

The earl tried to kiss Aurora's hand. "Behold me on my knees, as you prophesied," he said. He sounded a trifle light-headed, and Aurora wondered if his wound had started to bleed again.

"This is no time for funning, my lord," she cried. "Oh, the folly of it all! Here, hold on to my shoulder. Let me support you to the sofa. I marvel how you contrived to drive all this distance. You should have at least taken your groom."

She supported him to the sofa, and he sank on to it gratefully. The next moment he slumped back, exceedingly pale, his eyes closed.

"He has swooned!" Priscilla cried upon reentering the room, and nearly dropped the tray with glasses and the decanter of brandy.

"Well, don't you swoon too. Go fetch the doctor," commanded Aurora, sending her out again, although her own hand trembled as she poured some liquor into a glass and pressed it to the earl's lips. He stirred a little and moaned.

"Drink this, and don't move! Don't raise your arms," ordered Aurora, holding the glass to his lips.

The earl obeyed meekly, but after a few swallows he pushed the glass away. He seemed to have recovered somewhat. "Miss Marshingham—Aurora—" he began.

"Pray don't talk. Save your strength till the doctor arrives."

"Don't tell me what to do. I'm not on my deathbed yet,"

he snapped. He tried to possess himself of her hand once more.

Aurora stamped her foot again. "Will you be still, my lord! I'm endeavoring to ascertain if the wound has opened. I believe I see a red spot on your waistcoat."

The earl glanced down. "Damnation! I believe you are right. But it doesn't signify. It's just a drop. Ma'am—Miss Marshingham—I must—I must beg you to listen to me. You may do with me what you will afterward—throw me out or fetch the doctor. But listen to me you must!" His voice was full of urgency and his chest was heaving.

"Oh, very well, say your piece, or you shall fret yourself into a worse fever," Aurora agreed.

"Pray sit down beside me. It is difficult for me to speak, craning my neck."

"Very well." Aurora seated herself on the sofa. "But I must staunch the bleeding first."

"No. Wait for the sawbones to do it. It's not bleeding much.

"Aurora," the earl continued, "Style revealed to me the truth about your relationship with him. I wish I had known the whole. I wish you had told me—that you were just helping Lavinia out of a fix by pretending to be with Style at that masquerade."

"I don't tattle, my lord. Lady Lanville requested my help, and I promised it. I don't go back on my word. In any case, you never believe anything I say."

The earl groaned in despair. "I know. I have been guilty of that. And I deeply regret it. Pray accept my most profound and humble—"

"Oh, never humble," said Aurora.

"—apologies for my churlishness and my offensive conduct, and allow me to make amends."

"No amends are necessary," Aurora said stiffly.

"But you must allow me to make amends." The earl was getting excited again. "I've asked you this before and I'm asking you again—will you do me the honor of becoming my wife?"

"What!" Aurora snatched her hand away. "And you have the effrontery to insult me once more with your proposal!"

The earl's anger flared. "You have said that before. And

I ask again, is it an insult to bestow my name and my not inconsiderable fortune on a penniless girl?"

"Who became penniless through your contrivances?" Aurora finished for him.

"Through my unwitting neglect," corrected the earl. His face was flushed. "I wish you to become my wife. You must allow me to make amends."

Aurora's heart contracted painfully. She could have cried with vexation. "I realize it would be a great honor to become my Lady Roxton, yet I do not desire that honor, and I must decline your lordship's generous offer. A marriage should be founded at least on mutual respect. There is none on either side. I am only surprised that you feel your guilt so deeply you would offer marriage to me, whom you loathe and despise."

"No! That is no longer true!" cried the earl in a tortured voice. "It was never true! I only *thought* I hated you. But I didn't. I loved you!"

"What!" Aurora jumped to her feet. "My lord, this has gone far enough. You showed me utter contempt, you showered me with the worst possible insults you could think of— and you call *that* love! God spare me from a love like that!"

"But it is true, all perfectly true," the earl exclaimed. "Oh, yes, I hated you, or so I thought. But it wasn't really you I hated. I hated myself more. For while thinking the worst of you, I could not help loving and desiring you at the same time. I could not get you out of my mind. And it drove me to distraction! The thought that you were Style's mistress infuriated me and stirred such demons of jealousy in me as I had never experienced before. It made me wish to put a period to his existence so as to remove him from your reach!"

Aurora's cheeks became suffused with red. "I cannot believe it! It—it cannot be true."

"But it is true! Why do you think I changed my mind about that ridiculous duel when I saw you leaving his house?" the earl asked. "I wanted to kill him so that you would not belong to him any more."

"But, my lord, this is preposterous." Aurora felt light-headed.

"Preposterous, is it? To love someone to distraction? To

love someone in spite of thinking that person unworthy of one's love? And then—then on discovering that one was mistaken...

"Aurora, when Style told me the truth about that masquerade and about you, I could not wait a moment longer. I had to see you immediately. He told me—he gave me hope that—that you might be inclined to forgive—"

"Lord Style should not meddle in what is none of his concern," said Aurora with asperity, but her heart was pounding and a feeling of exultation was lifting her to the very heights of delight. He loved her even when he thought her base. Was that possible...?

She gazed into his upturned, entreating eyes and what she read there seemed to reassure her. She caught her breath. She had hoped secretly, without owning it to herself, that perhaps in time he might lose his contempt for her and might somehow grow to like her. But this...

"Aurora, will you forgive me and marry me? Tell me quickly, for I fear I may swoon again. And I must know, I *must*."

Aurora recollected his injury. "Your wound!" she exclaimed. "Let me place a pad on your wound."

His fingers gripped her wrist and, in spite of his weakness, held on fast. "Tell me first if you forgive me."

"Yes, yes, I forgive you. Only let me attend to this wound. Perhaps you ought to have more brandy."

"Will you marry me?"

"My lord, you must reconsider. You are not yourself. When you are restored to full health once more, you might think better of your rash proposal."

"It is not a rash proposal," the earl insisted. "I wished to marry you from the first moment I laid eyes on you. Only I was such a nodcock I didn't realize it at once."

"But, my lord—"

"Will you marry me?" the earl roared. "No, by God! I will not ask you any more. I have never been reduced to begging, and I will not do so now. You shall marry me, whether you like it or not." And with the last remnant of strength the earl pulled Aurora to his side and took her in his arms. Regardless of his weakness and his wound, his lips pressed to her lips in a hot, lingering kiss.

Feeling every fiber of her body respond to his passion, Aurora forgot his insults and her pride, forgot everything in that one exquisite moment of rapture. But soon his arms began to tire, and he pushed her gently away from him. "Now tell me that you still don't wish to marry me," he said in a voice in which wonder mixed with delight.

"I suppose if I told you I don't wish it, you would not believe me," said Aurora, but without much protest.

"No, I would not. For it would not be true. Now, give me your answer quickly, before somebody interrupts us. I think I hear hoofbeats. Will you marry me?"

"Your wound—it's bleeding more."

"Damn and blast the wound! Will you answer me now?"

"Yes, yes. Only pray do not excite yourself. Oh, dear, where is that doctor? Oh, I don't know whether to laugh or to cry. Oh, my darling!" Suddenly she was cradling his weary head on her shoulder. "Of course I will marry you. I love you so, you foolish, arrogant, odious man."

The earl lifted his head. "We shall suit very well, my beautiful, masterful termagant. We understand each other perfectly." And then, overcome by exhaustion and relief, he relaxed against her shoulder, closing his eyes, while a smile of contentment played upon his lips.

WHAT READERS SAY ABOUT
SECOND CHANCE AT LOVE

"SECOND CHANCE AT LOVE is fantastic."
—*J. L., Greenville, South Carolina**

"SECOND CHANCE AT LOVE has all the romance of the big novels."
—*L. W., Oak Grove, Missouri**

"You deserve a standing ovation!"
—*S. C., Birch Run, Michigan**

"Thank you for putting out this type of story. Love and passion have no time limits. I look forward to more of these good books."
—*E. G., Huntsville, Alabama**

"Thank you for your excellent series of books. Our book stores receive their monthly selections between the second and third week of every month. Please believe me when I say they have a frantic female calling them every day until they get your books in."
—*C. Y., Sacramento, California**

"I have become addicted to the SECOND CHANCE AT LOVE books...You can be very proud of these books....I look forward to them each month."
—*D. A., Floral City, Florida**

"I have enjoyed every one of your SECOND CHANCE AT LOVE books. Reading them is like eating potato chips, once you start you just can't stop."
—*L. S., Kenosha, Wisconsin**

"I consider your SECOND CHANCE AT LOVE books the best on the market."
—*D. S., Redmond, Washington**

*Names and addresses available upon request